FILM CRITICS PRAISE

BILLY JACK

"The 'counterculture' by and large has not fared well in the movies. Co-opted, commercialized and corrupted, the mysterious but palpable cultural shift in America often seems on the screen like the private gig of a few personalities . . . Into this state of affairs BILLY JACK RIDES with a real sense of refreshment."

Jack Kroll, *Newsweek* Magazine

"A popular line on BILLY JACK is that it preaches pacifism while displaying violence, whereas, to me, its purpose is to try to understand and reconcile these contrasting forces in American life . . . BILLY JACK is the nicest surprise of the year."

Stuart Byron, *The Village VOICE*

| Tom Laughlin | as | Billy Jack |
| Delores Taylor | as | Jean Roberts |

BILLY JACK
TECHNICOLOR®
STARRING

| Clark Howat | as | Sheriff Cole |

COSTARRING

Bert Freed	as	Posner
Julie Webb	as	Barbara
Ken Tobey	as	Deputy
Victor Izay	as	Doctor

WITH

Debbie Schock	as	Kit
Stan Rice	as	Martin
Teresa Kelly	as	Carol
Katy Moffatt	as	Maria
Susan Foster	as	Cindy
Paul Bruce	as	Councilman
Lynn Baker	as	Sarah
Susan Sosa	as	Sunshine
David Roya	as	Bernard
Gwen Smith	as	Angela
John McClure	as	Dinosaur
Cissie Colpitts	as	Miss Eyelashes

A NATIONAL STUDENT FILM

CREDITS

BROS.
SERVICE PRESENTS

Produced by Mary Rose Solti

Directed by T. C. Frank

Screenplay by Frank and Teresa Christina

Directors of Photography F. Koenekamp,
   A.S.C.; Jn. Stephens

Sound Effects by Edit International Ltd.

Edited by Larry Heath & Marion Rothman

Production Supervisor Linda Morrow

Titles and Opticals by Pacific Title

Music Editor Else Blangsted

Production Manager Wes McAfee

Publicist Don Prince

Associate Producers Ed Haldeman; Earl D. Elliott

Music Composed and Conducted by Mundell Lowe

"One Tin Soldier" Performed by Coven
   Written by Dennis Lambert; B. Potter

Indian Snake Ceremony, Rolling Thunder of
   Shoshone Nation

The Wokova Friendship Dance,
   Andy Vidovich of Paiute Nation

Hapkido Karate, Bon Soo Han of Korea

Asst. Directors M. Dmytryk; Jos. E. Rickards

CORPORATION PRODUCTION

BILLY JACK

Frank and Teresa Christina

AVON
PUBLISHERS OF BARD, CAMELOT, DISCUS, EQUINOX AND FLARE BOOKS

This Avon edition is the first publication
of *BILLY JACK* in book form.

AVON BOOKS
A division of
The Hearst Corporation
959 Eighth Avenue
New York, New York 10019

First Avon Printing, March, 1973
Seventh Printing, July, 1974

Printed in the U.S.A.

INTRODUCTION

"How do I account for the phenomenal success of *Billy Jack*?"*

Every time either I or Delores Taylor is asked that question we think back to that night in Prescott, Arizona, when we were scouting locations one month before the filming of the picture began.

It was late at night. The airport was very small. A bright Shell sign illuminated by a spot light was the most visible landmark in front of the tiny airport.

Some of our group noticed that an owl had suddenly flown down into the bright glare of the spot light and perched on the Shell sign.

This is highly unusual for an owl.

The Navajo regard the owl as a messenger of death. Though my crew pretended to scoff at all such superstitions, none of them was about to get on the airplane that was due in any moment.

In our party was a friend who had helped us during this scouting trip. He was an Iroquois who had had a dream years before. It had instructed him to walk to the land of the Hopis and to assist them as a messenger. Whenever we went to scout a town, while some of us were talking to the town officials, my Indian friend would disappear for a day or two and talk with the people in the Indian community to ask for their permission to shoot in that area. If we received permission from the civic officials but not from the Indians, we would not shoot there.

Quietly my Indian friend Craig went out, sat in a dark part of a parking lot, spread out his medicine, and smoked. I sat behind him for a long time until he motioned for me to come forward.

---

* *Billy Jack* has become one of the most remarkable box office successes of all time. More people have seen *Billy Jack* four to five times during its first release than any picture in history; it has played longer in more cities and towns across the United States than any picture in history except *The Sound of Music.*

I asked him if we should get on the plane.

He informed me that it would be all right. He has often tried to convince the Navajos that the owl is not always a messenger of death, but can be a messenger of other news as well. In this case, he said the owl had come to give me a message, which was:

First, that the picture we were about to make (*Billy Jack*) was going to do more good for the youth of America than any picture in recent times. The second part, however, told of demons who did not want this message to reach the American people and consequently I would be put through unbelievable hell for the next three years as they tried to keep the picture from being made.

At the time, because I respect things that come from the other world, I was intensely interested in the message, but it did not make a great deal of sense to me.

You must understand the situation.

We were ready to make a motion picture. After a long period of planning we were finally about to realize a dream, and we were ecstatic about starting on this new project. This talk of obstacles did not make sense to me.

Now that the three years are over—almost to the month —I realize how remarkably prophetic Craig's words to me were that night.

In the first place, *Billy Jack* did indeed become a most influential and successful picture with the young people of America, making it the greatest youth culture picture of our times.

Delores and I are keenly aware that such success has little to do with us. No film maker is so skillful he can produce a picture that so deeply burns its way into the collective consciousness of a people at will.

Secondly, the problems that beset us from the beginning of *Billy Jack* would, in itself, make a complete book.

We began making the picture under the auspices of American International Pictures with total and complete creative control as an absolute requisite of our deal. Within the first week of shooting, the head of American International Pictures left the country. Subsequent attempts were made to interfere with our creative relationship, followed by contracts which fundamentally altered the agreement. Two weeks later, our difficulties unresolved, I threatened to close down the company and return home rather than proceed under the changed arrangement. I was warned by those close to me that such an action had never before been done and that it would ruin me as a director in Hollywood.

Delores and I spent a long night of agonized appraisal and decided that it was more important that we remain true to our inspirations than work again in Hollywood, so we closed the company down and came home to Los Angeles.

For four months the legal hassles went on, and finally we worked out an amicable settlement with American International and received the rights to our picture.

Then we made a deal with Joe Levine of Avco Embassy, and for the next six weeks we prepared to produce the picture while the contracts were being drawn. Then, on the day of the signing, Avco Embassy—without any explanation to this day—refused to sign. I had to tell all the cast and crew who were signed, as well as all the creditors whom I had been stalling with the promise of paying them as soon as we signed the contract that I was once again broke and out of business.

After that we formed a relationship with Twentieth Century–Fox and managed to get the picture into production again by April, 1970.

A key element to our new deal was that Twentieth Century–Fox had no rights in the picture until we completed it. Before the delivery date we were free to make the picture exactly as we saw fit.

Throughout the shooting there were many strange and unexplained difficulties, but I cannot elaborate on them in this brief introduction. They ranged from people withdrawing permission to shoot in places at the last moment, to cameras being out of focus for a whole day's work, to one of the teen-age girls of the cast behaving as if she were "possessed" and having a hysterical breakdown in a bathroom until an Indian medicine man was called and, with the assistance of a special sacred sunrise ceremony to the Sun, calmed her. Some of the Indians believed "bad demons" were invading the young and harassing the company.

After slugging through hundreds of such problems we were ready to edit and finish the picture.

Richard Zanuck, then head of Twentieth Century–Fox, had no right under the terms of our contract to edit the film until after I had delivered it to him *en toto*. During the editing he had two meetings with me. At this time he wanted to cut out all the scenes essential to the development of the ambience that we felt was necessary for the picture. He wanted to cut out the "God is Black" improvisational scene, the marihuana improvisational scene, the city council session, and the robbery in the park, among others. I was appalled, so he agreed to let me finish it exactly my way, after which we would test the picture with three previews and be guided by the response of the audience. His staff insisted we preview it in Orange County, which is notorious as an ultraconservative element of Los Angeles, to see how offensive these scenes would be. I agreed.

Before I could finish editing, however, I was stunned to receive a message from someone at Fox which said that Fox was arranging to take my negative from the laboratory vault—something which they had absolutely no right to do. To our shock we found that the film had been taken from the vault and we no longer had access to our own picture. Such is Hollywood.

We immediately took the sound track from the sound laboratory and left Twentieth Century–Fox with 250,000 feet of film, half of which was improvised and did not match the script. They had no sound track to use with the picture.

Delores and I took a long week off to decide what to do.

We knew that if the film were released in the manner Fox wanted, it would totally destroy the message of the picture and become nothing more than an action melodrama. In addition, it would not only destroy the picture and its message, but it would seriously destroy our thrust for creative freedom.

Let me expain that. The only way a film maker can have total creative freedom over his artistic work is to make the film with his own money or to get in a position where he can use other people's money without their having any control over the artistic product. The only way he can do that is by developing a track record of successful pictures proving he has a "nose" for audiences which will return a profit on his pictures.

Investors couldn't care less about the content of the picture. They are only interested in receiving their money back with a profit. It is an ugly fact of life that a film maker cannot practice his craft unless he has thousand of dollars of other people's money. He does not have the freedom of a writer, a poet, or a painter. We knew that letting Fox put the picture out the way they intended would destroy the message and, thereby, result in disaster at the box office, destroying the track record we had built up so successfully with our last movie, *Born Losers*, which is still one of the top grossing films in American International Pictures' history.

From the standpoint of philosophical and artistic integrity, as well as from the standpoint of building our freedom to keep making our "message" pictures, Delores and I felt that to let Fox go ahead and cut the picture their way would be to destroy everything we were trying to build. So we concluded that if the film had to be destroyed, we would do it. Therefore, we authorized our attorneys to file suit against Twentieth Century–Fox. We knew this would tie the picture up in the courts for years—something Fox counted on—and therefore virtually would kill *Billy Jack* forever. In addition, we asked that word be sent to Fox that we would send them one erased reel of tape a week until the sound track was totally destroyed, and which could never be replaced.

At that point, Fox caved in and gave us a very limited period of time to raise just under one million dollars to buy the picture back.

Without any money and with creditors hounding us for hundreds of thousands of dollars, we managed to finish the picture, raise the money, and buy out Fox. Instead of this being a happy ending, it was only the beginning of new trials, for when we made an arrangement with Warner Bros. to release the picture, the worst phase of our troubles began.

That phase can best be summed up by the fact that we have filed a $51 million dollar antitrust lawsuit against Warner Bros. in the state and federal courts.

It is no secret. It was our contention that Warner Bros. did not believe in the picture and dumped down on it . . . only to have it catch on all by itself and continue to grow and build until it becomes one of the weirdest success stories in modern cinema history.

Looking back on it—the number of times that Delores and I were broke, including the time when our furniture was repossessed and our children were sleeping on the floor; the promises made and inexplicably broken; and the personal collapse that Delores and I suffered individually, to the point where we almost wanted to leave the business because of what was happening to us—the prophecy of the owl regarding the obstacles seems amazing.

The picture was a success, and the three years were unbelievable hell!

I would like to elaborate further on the Indians' influence in the picture, but space permits only hinting at them.

I could tell how adamant I was, insisting on using the black Navajo hat when Delores, my children, and all of those whom I trust told me not to because I looked silly in it . . . yet, for some strange reason, I had to wear it. Months later, after almost completing the shooting of the picture, I met the Indian leader Wovoka's son-in-law, a Paiute Indian named Andy Vidovich, who showed me the first snapshot I ever saw of Wovoka. I literally felt goose bumps as I saw upon Wovoka's head the black Navajo hat that I wore in the movie.

How Andy Vidovich came to us was another amazing story.

After we had shot the first part of the picture and had been closed down for four months we went into Santa Fe, New Mexico, for the final shooting. An Indian who had lived at the Taos pueblo came to me and asked to see the script. He called excitedly a few hours later and told me that the script contained elements of the ghost religion. I had no idea what that was and asked if he could explain. He said he didn't know a great deal about it, but would check into it. He did know that it had started with a Paiute Indian named Wovoka and was the religion that was responsible for the massacre at Wounded Knee.

Within an hour after I hung up a call came to me in Santa Fe from my Iroquois friend who was that moment on the Hoopa reservation in Northern California. He said he just had a feeling to call and see how things were going. I mentioned to him the new information regarding Wovoka and he told me that I must immediately call Andy Vidovich, who was not only Wovoka's son-in-law, but was his spiritual heir and who could tell me all about Wovoka's teaching. This was especially important because Andy felt Wovoka's teaching has been badly misinterpreted in all the history books, and he was very anxious to get the true message out before he died because he was a very old man.

I called Andy Vidovich but his hearing was gone and he could not understand me on the phone. He certainly had no idea what our movie was or who I was. An interesting series of events developed. I asked Andy Vidovich if he would fly to New Mexico for I needed him for the next day's shooting. He agreed!

Andy Vidovich had never flown in an airplane before in his life. He was deathly terrified of them. During World War

II his son was a Flying Tiger and the most important thing in Andy's life, yet he would never get in an airplane with him. But here he was getting on a small plane in Nevada, flying into Elko, on a larger plane to Reno, then to Los Angeles, then to Albuquerque. He had no idea when he arrived who we were or what our movie was about or why we needed him.

All of the things he taught us about Wovoka were then added to the script spontaneously that day.

I wish there were time here to go into how Wovoka's teaching had been distorted by those who used its power and message as a means for creating destruction and war. At one time Wovoka met with Sitting Bull and told him that if the Lakota (Sioux) continued to use the medicine for destructive purposes Sitting Bull would be killed at the hands of his own people, and that the Sioux would suffer worse than any tribe. Many of the Plains Indians continued to use the religion in its negative form, feeling that for the first time they had the power to overcome the white man's savage invasion and rape of his land, and so Wovoka's words were not heeded. What happened to Sitting Bull and the Lakota is history.

I could talk about the medicine man of the Shoshones, John "Rolling Thunder" Pope, who underwent the sacred snake ceremony in the picture. He came to us to tell us that we should put this in the picture (in a disguised form) and was present during the entire shooting of the ceremony, which he supervised very closely.

There were other Indians who had dreams or inspirations and came to us during the shooting to help guide us in the making of the picture.

Sometime in the future, perhaps, we will put it all down in great detail. In the meantime, I cannot help looking back on that night in Prescott when the owl alighted and predicted the impact of the picture on young people as well as the difficulties we would encounter. Only now do we realize how significant and symbolical that beginning was.

As I go through the jungle of Hollywood today, with all the studio heads and their lawyers pontificating in their cigar filled rooms, flanked by their computer executives and black suited banker advisors, who complain about what is wrong with audiences and how they have changed, I cannot help wishing they were more in tune with that other world —the world where all real creative artists enter and spend time before returning to the collective cultural canon with their artistic vision. This is the same world that all traditional people, from the Laps in Finland to the young Americans, from the Jungians to the Eastern mystics, and especially the American Indian know about but don't often share with outsiders for fear of ridicule.

It is the "message" of this world, or at least its vibrations, that has fascinated man from the first fall. It is the lucky film-maker who, by the gift of his guide, taps into this world and truly makes the world of cinema live again, satisfying both his inner inspirations and his audiences, and moves us all one tiny step further into consciousness.

That, to me, is what films—and *Billy Jack*—is all about. We thank all of you—from both worlds—for letting us play a part in bringing *Billy Jack* to visible life.

We especially thank the owl.

Most of all, we thank *Billy Jack!*

Tom Laughlin
Delores Taylor

STREET EXTERIOR DAY

A police car pulls out onto a deserted city street and proceeds along the drab main thoroughfare.

> **JEAN**
> (*voice over*)
> *There were probably no two people on this earth more opposite from each other than myself and Billy Jack and, now that I look back on it, it's hard to believe that the chain of events that would first bring us so close together and then end up in so much tragedy and bloodshed could begin with an early Saturday morning drive by Sheriff Cole over to his deputy's house.*

The police car, with Sheriff Cole at the wheel, turns onto a residential street, lined with modest frame houses, bleak in the cold morning sun.

Mike, the deputy, is about to enter his car, parked on the street in front of his house.

> **MIKE**
> *Good morning, Cole. What brings you out this hour?*

> **COLE**
> (*from his car*)
> *They found your daughter.*

> **MIKE**
> *Oh, where? Haight Ashbury again?*

> **COLE**
> *Yeah. They're flying her into Phoenix. You want to take my car and go down and get her?*

MIKE
When?

COLE
Now.

MIKE
Oh I can't, dammit. Posner just called and told me to be out at Box Canyon in half an hour.

COLE
It's illegal for anyone to hunt wild mustang, Mike, especially a deputy sheriff, you know that.

MIKE
I know. I also know that when Posner says jump, a lot of people in this town have to jump, including me.

COLE
What do you want to do about Barbara?

MIKE
(hesitates)
Look, Cole, I'll try to get back before she gets here.

Mike gets in his car.

COLE
Say, Mike . . . .

MIKE
Yeah.

COLE
How much are the dog food companies paying for mustang meat now?

MIKE
Six cents a pound. Why?

COLE
Oh nothing. I was just wondering if Barbara would think it was worth it.

As Sheriff Cole drives away, the theme "One Tin Soldier" begins as the camera pans over the mountain.
The titles begin over the music.

ONE TIN SOLDIER
Listen children to a story
That was written long ago
'Bout a kingdom on a mountain
And a valley far below
On the mountain was the treasure
Buried deep beneath the stone
In the valley people swore
They'd have it for their very own
Go ahead and hate your neighbor
Go ahead and cheat a friend
Do it in the name of Heaven
You can justify it in the end
There won't be any trumpets blowing
Come the judgment day
On the bloody morning after
One tin soldier rides away

So the people of the valley
Sent a message on the hill
Asking for the buried treasure
Tons of gold for which they'd kill
Came an answer from the kingdom
With our brothers we will share
All the secrets of our mountain
All the riches buried there
Now the valley cried with anger
Mount your horses draw your swords
And they killed the mountain people
So they won their just reward
Now they stood beside the treasure
On the mountain dark and red
Turned the stone and looked beneath it

15

Peace on earth was all it said
Go ahead and hate your neighbor
Go ahead and cheat a friend
Do it in the name of heaven
You can justify it in the end
There won't be any trumpets blowing
Come the judgment day
On the bloody morning after
One tin soldier rides away

Go ahead and hate your neighbor
Go ahead and cheat a friend
Do it in the name of heaven
You can justify it in the end
There won't be any trumpets blowing
Come the judgment day
On the bloody morning after
One tin soldier rides away

Unaware mustangs are thrown into confusion by the sudden approach of the hunters on horseback. The mustangs plunge in terror before the horsemen, some stumbling and rolling among the loose rock of a precipice. The horses race in terror through a stream, the hunters chasing relentlessly, shouting harsh commands and whipping their lariats in the air. Eventually, the mustangs are encircled and herded into a crudely fenced enclosure.

The exhausted horses move in restless apprehension as the horsemen come to a stop outside the corral. As the group of men chasing the horses rides up, Bernard Posner jumps in a truck near the corral.

MIKE
(raising a rifle)
Would you like the first shot, Mr. Posner?

POSNER
Thanks, Mike, I'll let Bernard have that.

Posner dismounts, walks to Bernard and opens the door of the truck.

POSNER
(quietly, so as not to be overheard by the men)
*Come on now, Bernard, get your ass up out of that
truck. Get up there and start shooting.*

BERNARD
(reluctantly)
Please dad, you know I can't shoot.

POSNER
I said now!

Bernard gets out and climbs on top of the truck. Posner
hands him a rifle. Bernard raises the rifle as if to aim, then
hesitates.

POSNER
Shoot! Shoot, damn you!

BERNARD
I can't.

Bernard throws the rifle back at Posner.

POSNER
All right, Mike. Start shooting.

The men release their safetys and take aim, but hesitate as
they sense something strange and mysterious in the air.
They look around uncomfortably. There is a rustling in
the trees behind them and a shadow appears. Finally we
see Billy Jack emerge, slowly riding his horse from the
wooded area into the clearing toward the men.

MIKE
I knew he'd find us.

POSNER
Good morning, Billy.

BILLY
You're illegally on Indian land.

POSNER
I'm sorry about that. I guess we just got caught up in the chase and crossed over without knowing it.

BILLY
(calmly)
You're a liar.

POSNER
We got the law here, Billy Jack.

BILLY
When policemen break the law, then there isn't any law, just a fight for survival.

MIKE
Uh, Mr. Posner, I got no authority on a federal Indian reservation.

One of the men picks up his rifle, Billy Jack spins and shoots at him.

BILLY
Drop it or die. On this reservation I am the law. So I'll tell you this just once. Have your men drop their guns and you can leave quietly.

POSNER
You're making a mistake.

BILLY
I've made them before.

MAN
We've got him outnumbered, Mr. Posner.

BILLY
You know me, Posner, you know my meaning.

Posner drops his rifle.

POSNER
Drop them.

The others drop their guns, turn and ride away. Billy Jack releases the horses, moves among them on horseback, watching as they gallop to freedom.

JEAN
(v.o.)
All any of the townspeople knew about Billy Jack was that he was a half-breed, a war hero who hated the war and turned his back on society by returning to the reservation where he watched over the Indians, the wild horses, and the kids at my school. No one even knew where he lived, somewhere way back in the ancient ruins with an old holy man who was teaching him for a sacred initiation ceremony.

Barbara is brought to her house by Sheriff Cole. Mike is outside.

Barbara gets out of the car and goes quickly up the walk. Mike reaches out for her as she approaches.

MIKE
How are you, sweetie?

Barbara pushes past him and walks into the house. Mike follows her. She sits on the couch and stares sullenly, straight ahead into space.

MIKE
My first instinct is to beat the hell out of you, you know that, don't you? But it probably wouldn't do any good, would it? Bet you're hungry. Can I fix you something to eat, Barb? How long since you last eaten?

BARBARA
(quietly)
Two days.

MIKE
Two days! No wonder you don't look well.

BARBARA
I don't look well because I've got hepatitis and a goddamned abscessed tooth that's killing me.

MIKE
Well let's call the doctor.

Mike picks up the phone, his back to Barbara.

BARBARA
You can't call the doctor. He'll make me stay in the hospital.

MIKE
I know, but that's the only way to cure hepatitis.

BARBARA
Not because of hepatitis, because of the baby.

MIKE
What baby?

BARBARA
The "it" baby. I'm pregnant.

MIKE
You're what?

BARBARA
Pregnant.

Mike looks stunned, drops the phone and turns to Barbara.

MIKE
I've been expecting this. How long?

BARBARA
Oh, maybe six weeks.

MIKE
All right, where's the father?

BARBARA
Where's the father? That's funny, I don't even know who the father is.

MIKE
What's that supposed to mean?

BARBARA
(bitterly)
It means, concerned father, that I was passed around by so many of those phony maharishi types who kept telling me that love is beautiful and all that bullshit ... in other words, concerned father, I got balled by so many guys I don't know if the father's going to be white, Indian, Mexican, or black!

Mike walks to the couch, stands over her in rage and punches her hard in the face.

LAKESIDE   EXTERIOR   DAY

Barbara is lying asleep on the ground, as Billy Jack rides through high, dry grass and sights her. Her face is bruised and swollen. Billy dismounts and goes to her. He leans over and gently shakes her shoulder.

BILLY
Hey, hey, miss. Hey, come on, wake up.

DOCTOR'S OFFICE   INTERIOR   DAY

The doctor comes out of the examining room. Barbara is lying on a table in the background. Sheriff Cole and Billy are waiting in the hallway.

DOCTOR
Well, she's a pretty sick girl but nothing that a lot of bed rest won't cure. The question now is what are

21

*we going to do with her? Another beating like that
and she'll lose that baby.*

COLE
Be the best thing that could happen.

DOCTOR
Cole!

COLE
All right. Billy, anyone see you bring her in here?

Billy shakes his head.

DOCTOR
Why? What do you have in mind?

COLE
*Well, we can't take her home and Posner would pro-
tect her father against anything we could do. We
sure can't hide her anywhere around town, so . . . .*

BILLY
So you want me to hide her out at the school.

COLE
Yeah. At least until she gets well.

BARBARA
I ain't going to no damned school.

They turn toward Barbara and the doctor goes back into
her room.

DOCTOR
*Well, it's either that or go back to your father.
Besides this isn't an ordinary school, it's a very pro-
gressive school out at the reservation run by a very
remarkable woman. You'll like her.*

BARBARA
The person hasn't been born I'd like.

BILLY
What is her father going to do when he finds out that she's out there?

COLE
He thinks she ran away. Nobody here's going to tell him any different.

CORRAL EXTERIOR DAY

Jean is on horseback in a corraled area at the school. The students watch as Kit rides her horse through a barrel race course.

Sheriff Cole, the doctor, and Barbara drive up in a car. Billy drives up in the jeep.

JEAN
Turn now! Come in much wider! If you want to win, Kit, you gotta do better than eighteen seconds.

KIT
Gee, I just can't seem to come in close enough? Can you show me again?

Jean runs the course expertly as the kids cheer. Barbara watches from the car.

BARBARA
What are they doing?

DOCTOR
Probably teaching some of the kids how to barrel race.

COLE
Anything any kid wants to learn, they try to teach it to them here.

DOCTOR
I told you this was a different kind of school.

23

SCHOOL GROUNDS EXTERIOR DAY

Jean describes the school as Barbara follows unenthusiastically. The camera shows us students engaged in various activities: a group seated cross-legged, chanting, under a massive granite statue of three Indian drummers; a pop group performing outdoors under trees; weavers working in the crafts room; young artists absorbed in painting; and a yoga group practicing meditation.

> **JEAN**
> *(v.o.)*
> *When I took over this school out here at the reservation, I knew there would be trouble. First because I opened it up to any kid with a problem, black, white, Indian, Chicano, who could come anytime they wanted, stay as long as they wanted, and leave when they wanted—no questions asked. Then people became even more hostile when I announced that there would be only three rules: no drugs; everyone had to carry his own load; and everyone had to get turned on by creating something, anything, whether it be weaving a blanket, making a film, or doing a painting, preferably something that made one proud of one's own heritage and past. Or by being involved in such strange things as yoga meditation.*

SCHOOL INTERIOR DAY

> **YOGA TEACHER**
> *Keep your eyes focused on the third point.*

> **JEAN**
> *(v.o.)*
> *Or psychodrama and role playing, things that the townspeople could never understand.*

A group of students are involved in role-playing. Barbara is watching off to the side. Jean approaches the leaders of the group.

JEAN
You guys are my last chance. Do you think you can do anything with her?

ED
Sure, okay, no problem. Let's hold it for just a minute, okay. Okay, everybody, this is Barbara. She's going to be working with us for a while and instead of going through a lot of introductions why don't we just get to know each other by getting into another scene.

KIT
Why don't we do one of those role playing things where we send her out of the room and she has to come back and figure out what's going on and who you are.

ED
Good idea. All you have to do is come into the scene and discover who you are as the scene progresses.

BARBARA
I can't.

STUDENTS
Why not?

BARBARA
The reason I'm here is because I'm knocked up.

BOY
Congratulations.

GIRL
That's great, let's just do one about her being pregnant, that's all.

Cindy takes Barbara out of the room.

ED
All right then, let's get it together.

BOY
I got a good one.

ED
Okay.

BOY
How about if the world is really fucked up and really needs a new savior and she's going to give birth to it.

ALL
Okay ... great ... yeah, that's good.

ED
Okay, now let's rap it out. What happens?

GIRL
A virgin birth, a second one.

ED
Okay, a virgin birth.

GIRL
But this one's going to be a modern one, it won't have to be like the old kind, like a hip Jesus.

ED
A hip Jesus, okay, let's do it.

BLACK BOY
I want to be the savior.

Cindy and Kit bring Barbara in and lay her on the floor as Jean watches.

BARBARA
What are you doing?

A black boy emerges from under a blanket at her feet.

KIT
Oh, that's beautiful, a black Jesus.

The kids are all gathered around discussing the end of the scene and Barbara is talking animatedly.

Jean watches, pleased, from across the room.

BARBARA
So they should crucify them and then the rest of us say, give us a sign before you die or give us the answer or something before you die or something, because he's dying on the cross.

ALL
What's the sign for the new religion?

The black boy lifts his fist in the black-power sign and all the others do the same.

SCHOOL CAFETERIA INTERIOR DAY

On the wall is a mural of a buffalo hunt. The room is filled with students engaged in conversation.

Sunshine and Carol enter and walk over to Jean and Billy's table.

SUNSHINE
Carol wrote a new song about her brother but she's too bashful to sing it.

JEAN
Will you go up and sing it for us?

CAROL
(shyly)
I don't want to.

JEAN
Oh, come on, don't be so bashful, you sing so well.

Cissie walks by. She has red hair, a huge bust, and is heavily made up.

BARBARA
What's her trip?

KIT
She's really out of it. She wears three pairs of false eyelashes and she thinks the world is Hollywood in the 1940's.

CINDY
She's just not quite right, I guess she doesn't have anyplace else to go.

KIT
The whole idea of doing your thing in the mess hall came from a visit somebody made to a Benedictine monastery and anybody who wants to read or sing, or just do anything at all, just gets up and does it.

Jean and Carol are up onstage.

JEAN
Carol has written us a new song about her brother.

CAROL
Two of them.

JEAN
(smiling)
I beg your pardon, two of them. Go ahead.

CAROL
(singing)
Just goin' off to the war tomorrow
Just goin' off to fight tomorrow
Just goin' off to lose his life tomorrow.

Why is there war
Why is there killing
Why is there fighting and killing
  Families and children

Just goin' off to the war tomorrow
Just goin' off to fight tomorrow
Just goin' off to lose his life tomorrow.

Why can't we have some peace
Why do they have to fight
Why can't we live in harmony
And give all men equal rights.

Johnnie died last Friday
I got the news today
The sergeant called and said
Your brother is dead

My heart stopped beating
My mind just went blank
I'll never forget that moment
When the sergeant said
*Your brother is dead.**

There is silence in the cafeteria when Carol finishes her song. Some of the girls are crying.
Martin goes over to Billy Jack's table and sits down.

MARTIN
When you go through that ceremony to be a brother to the snake, do you let the rattlesnake bite you?

BILLY
Uh huh.

MARTIN
Over and over?

*Words and music by **Teresa Kelly**.
Sung by Teresa **Kelly**.

BILLY
Uh huh.

MARTIN
Could I be your apprentice and help learn the purification part?

BILLY
In order to be an apprentice you have to be able to strip yourself of your greed and your ego trips in order to let the spirit enter into you.

MARTIN
My grandmother was a Kachina. They say the spider woman came and worked through my grandfather. He was a medicine man.

The singing begins in the background, led by Carol and Jean up on the stage.

BILLY
(watching Martin intently)
Do you believe in the spirit?

MARTIN
One night when I was a boy one came and left the bow and arrow on my bed.

BILLY
Most people think that's a bunch of crap.

MARTIN
I don't.

Billy just looks at him.

ALL
(singing)
Look. Look to the mountain so green
Wish all your wishes there

Take a look around you
Everything is so clear.

Look, look to the mountain so clear
Wish all your wishes there
Don't tell your wish to anyone
Only Mister Mountain.

Look, look to the mountain so green
Wish all your wishes there
This place is just for you and me
Mister Mountain, the deer and bear.

Look, look to the mountain so clear
Keep it as green as you can
This is your treasure as long as you live
Believe me, I know.

Look, look to the mountain so green.*

Everyone applauds, and Jean hugs Carol.

DORMITORY   EXTERIOR   DAY

Billy Jack and Jean are walking toward his motorcycle parked under a tree. They stop to talk.

> **SARAH**
> (*singing - v. o.*)
> *Someone is laughing on the stair*
> *And tapping on the wall behind me*
> *I can hear them everywhere*
> *But when will Billy find me?*
> *When will Billy find me?*
>
> *People are running down the hall*
> *And walking on the floor above me*

*Words and music by Teresa Kelly.

I can hear them everywhere
But when will Billy love me?
When will Billy love me?

Oh, I could talk to them
Catch and throw a word or two
Perhaps I'd even share a kiss
But what good would it do?

People are running down the hall
And walking on the floor high above me
I can hear them everywhere
But when will Billy love me?
When will Billy love me?

Oh, I could talk to them
Catch and throw a word or two
Perhaps I'd even share a kiss
But what good would it do?

When will Billy love me?
When will Billy love me?
When will Billy love me?
When will Billy love me?
When will Billy love me?

BILLY
What are you so worried about?

SARAH
(v. o.)
And tapping on the wall behind me

JEAN
About the kids going into town tomorrow.

BILLY
Well why don't you just tell them that they can't go.

JEAN
I can't do that.

BILLY
Why not?

JEAN
Because they have to make their own decisions here, you know that,

DORMITORY EXTERIOR DAY

Sarah, Kit, Cindy and Barbara are on their beds singing and talking.

SARAH
(singing)
But when will Billy find me?
When will Billy find me?

BARBARA
Do they love each other?

Kit looks out the window and watches Jean and Billy for a moment.

KIT
Nobody knows.

SARAH
(singing)
Oh I could talk to them
Catch and throw a word or two
Perhaps I'd even share a kiss
But what good would it do?

DORMITORY INTERIOR DAY

JEAN
It's funny isn't it, how everybody in town's afraid of you. But I guess it's a good thing they are, 'cause if they weren't they'd hurt the school a lot more than they do now.

33

Billy sighs.

>**JEAN**
>*It's an awfully lonely life though, isn't it?*

>**BILLY**
>(gently placing his hand on the back of Jean's head)
>*What's gonna happen tomorrow is gonna happen. And all your worry in the world isn't gonna change that. Okay? Come on, smile.*

Jean shakes her head and then smiles.

>**BILLY**
>*Okay.*

>**JEAN**
>*Good-bye.*

Billy rides off on his motorcycle.

DORMITORY INTERIOR DAY

>**SARAH**
>(singing)
>*When will Billy love me*
>*When will Billy love me*
>*When will Billy love me*

TOWN EXTERIOR DAY
Students from the school are on their bus singing a freedom song. They are in a holiday mood, waving to the townspeople and raising their fingers in the peace signal.

As they drive through the streets, the townspeople stare at them strangely and hostilely.

The bus parks and the students pour out.

BARBERSHOP INTERIOR DAY

Cole sits in a chair on the stand, having his shoes shined.

CUSTOMER
Hey, Cole, when are you going to do something about those long-haired wierdos? Before or after they start burning their draft cards?

BARBER
No, he's waiting till some of our kids start going out there and smoking pot, ain't you, Cole?

COLE
Nope. Soon as I finish my shine I'm going out there and shoot three or four of them, show 'em who's boss.

BAR EXTERIOR DAY

A group of boys from the town are clustered outside a bar, staring and whistling at Cindy. They turn and go into the bar where Bernard is sitting.

BAR INTERIOR DAY

BOY
Is that class or is that class?

BERNARD
I've seen better.

BOY
Sure, Mr. Stud himself. He could pick up that chick just like that, couldn't you, Bernard?

DINOSAUR
Are you kidding? Of course he can handle her, can't you, Bernard?

BERNARD
Just put up the money, like say fifty bucks.

One of the boys puts the money on the counter.

BOY
Covered.

They laugh. Bernard is shocked. He didn't think they could possibly afford it. Now he has no choice but to go outside where he walks up to Cindy as she mails a letter. As she turns, she finds her way blocked by Bernard.

STREET EXTERIOR DAY

BERNARD
Howdy, my name's Bernard Posner.

CINDY
Oh really?

BERNARD
Really.

CINDY
Is that supposed to mean something?

BERNARD
Around these parts you hear the name Posner quite a bit.

CINDY
That's very interesting. You know you hear my name quite a bit, and not just around here either.

BERNARD
No fooling. What's your name?

CINDY
Up.

BERNARD
(laughing)
Up. That's an odd name. What's your last name?

CINDY
Yours. Up yours.

Cindy knocks his arm down and brushes past him, as the boys across the street roar with laughter.

Cindy walks over to a group of students standing across from the ice cream parlor.

> **CINDY**
> *Hey, why isn't everybody going in?*

> **MARTIN**
> *They're afraid to go in.*

> **CINDY**
> *Why?*

> **MARTIN**
> *Indians aren't allowed in some of the stores here.*

> **CINDY**
> *What do you mean "not allowed?" I don't see a sign.*

> **KIT**
> *Indians don't need a sign. They know damn well where they're not wanted.*

> **CINDY**
> *Then why are you going in?*

> **KIT**
> *'Cause I like ice cream.*

ICE CREAM PARLOR   INTERIOR   DAY

Cindy, Kit, Martin, Carol, and Sunshine enter the store. Harry, the man behind the counter is serving a couple of the town's kids ice cream cones.

> **MARTIN**
> *Can we have some ice cream please?*

Harry turns his back to them, and walks to the sink behind the counter.

MARTIN
Look, we'd like to buy some ice cream cones.

HARRY
Sorry I'm all out of cones.

Bernard and Dinosaur enter the store.

CINDY
You just served the kids ahead of us.

HARRY
Look, I told you, I'm all out of cones.

Cindy reaches over the counter and pulls a carton of cones out from under it.

CINDY
You're a liar.

HARRY
You're a smart little punk, aren't you.

Harry grabs the box of cones away from Cindy.

BERNARD
Hey, hold it, hold it. Come on, you guys, there's no need for all this violence. It's a simple problem really. Harry, look I know you worked hard to own your own store and you feel you should have a right to serve whoever you want to. Right?

HARRY
Right.

BERNARD
Okay. Well little Miss Up Yours here feels that if she wants you to serve her nonwhite friends you damn well better serve her nonwhite friends. That doesn't sound like an insurmountable problem. Hey, Dinosaur, bring me some of that flour over there.

The simple solution is simply to make Miss Up Yours' nonwhite friends white.

Bernard pours flour over Kit's head and down her face. Cindy rushes to help her, but Dinosaur grabs her.

CINDY
All right. All right.

BERNARD
(to Martin)
What's the matter, boy, you going to let the women do your fighting?

MARTIN
Come on, let's get out of here.

BERNARD
You know, I'm always suspicious of you pacifist types. That it's just a fancy way of covering up that you're yellow.

MARTIN
Please. This won't accomplish anything. We'll just leave.

BERNARD
Oh no. Our good deed's not done. As for the little one here . . . .

Martin goes to interfere and gets punched in the stomach by Dinosaur. He falls to the floor. Bernard then pours some more flour on Sunshine.

CAROL
Stop it!

Kit slaps Bernard in the face. Furious, he glares at her, then walks over and pours flour on Martin.

BERNARD
There now everybody is white, so Harry, why don't you serve all our friends an ice cream cone?

Billy Jack has pulled up in his jeep across the street, and crosses to enter the ice cream parlor.

Bernard looks in horror at the approaching Billy, now coming through the door.

> **BERNARD**
> *Remember, before you try anything, you're in our territory now with the Sheriff nearby.*

Billy stares for a long time at the kids with the flour poured over them.

> **BILLY**
> *(too calmly)*
> *Bernard, the Sheriff is out at the school.*

> **BERNARD**
> *Get my dad. And have someone get the Sheriff.*

One of the boys leaves. Billy looks around him. What he sees makes him angry, he sighs and looks out the window trying to gain control. Martin is still on the floor groaning.

> **BILLY**
> *(softly)*
> *Bernard ... oh ... I want you to know ... that I try. When Jean and the kids at the school tell me that I'm supposed to control my violent temper and be passive and nonviolent like they are, I try, I really try. But when I see this girl of such a beautiful spirit so degraded, and I see this boy that I love sprawled out by this big ape here . . . .*

Billy Jack picks Martin up from the floor.

> **BILLY**
> *... and this little girl who is so special to us that we call her God's little gift of sunshine and I think of the number of years she's going to have to carry in her memory the savagery of this idiotic moment of yours ... I just go ... berserk.*

40

The last word is practically a scream. Billy whirls around and hits Bernard in the stomach with a karate chop. He knocks down another boy who rushes to attack him, and chops Dinosaur up and throws him through the plate glass window. He looks for a moment, then walks over and kneels before the terrified Sunshine.

> **BILLY**
> *You hurt? Get in your eyes?*

Billy brushes the flour from Sunshine's face. Sunshine shakes her head.

> **BILLY**
> *A lot of stupid people in this world, aren't there? Sure you're all right? How come you don't smile? Huh? You do look kind of funny.*

Sunshine laughs and her fear goes away.

> **KIT**
> *You better go, they're going to kill you.*

> **BILLY**
> *You okay?*

Suddenly Billy seems to hear something.

TOWN EXTERIOR DAY

A hand is pulling a wire out of the carburetor of Billy's jeep.

ICE CREAM PARLOR INTERIOR DAY

Billy brushes the flour from Kit's face, then sits down slowly and deliberately removes his shoes and socks.

> **CAROL**
> *Don't go out there.*

CINDY
Nobody in town's gonna help you.

CAROL
Please don't go out there.

STREET   EXTERIOR   DAY

Billy Jack leaves the ice cream parlor, walks over to the jeep, lifts and looks under the hood, then turns and walks to the town square. As he walks, a dozen townsmen silently emerge, one by one, from behind the trees, and surround him.

Posner pulls up, leaves his car, and strides to the center of the ring of men and arrogantly faces Billy.

POSNER
Big Indian Chief, so special, so above the law. You think you can do just as you please. I told you you'd make a mistake and I'd be waiting.

MAN
Watch his feet, man, he can kill you with his feet.

POSNER
He can do anything he wants with his feet. You really think those Green Beret karate tricks gonna help you against all these boys?

BILLY
Well it doesn't look to me like I really have any choice now, does it?

POSNER
(laughing)
That's right, you don't.

BILLY
You know what I think I'm going to do then, just for the hell of it?

POSNER
Tell me.

BILLY
I'm going to take this right foot and I'm going to whop you on that side of your face—and you want to know something? There's not a damn thing you're going to be able to do about it.

POSNER
Really?

BILLY
(laughing)
Really.

So fast it can hardly be seen, Billy sweeps his leg in a flashing circle, catching Posner right in the face and chopping him to the ground.

Posner, his face in pain, screams out:

POSNER
Kill that Indian son of a bitch!

As the men come after him, Billy Jack cuts down one after the other with his karate blows. Finally one of the men strikes him on the back of his head with a stick, and as several of them hold him, he is beaten. As one of the men starts to throw a punch, his hand is stopped from behind by Sheriff Cole. Billy falls to the ground, his mouth bleeding.

COLE
Johnny, how you doing?
(walks a little farther)
Ben, hear you got a new foal out at your place. Howdy, Al. How's that new Olds working out? Pete ... well I think we've done enough damage for one day, don't you? Mike, take care of Billy Jack.

Mike gestures to some of the men to pick Billy up.

COLE
All right, let's everybody go home and take a hot bath.

HARRY
Wait a minute. Aren't you going to press charges?

Cole looks at the bodies on the ground and then sees Posner driving away in his car.

COLE
Where would I begin?

CORRAL EXTERIOR DAY

Several of the students watch as Martin saddles a horse.

SUNSHINE
Please, Martin, wait till they get back.

CAROL
Billy Jack said you should never practice alone, Martin, you know that.

MARTIN
Why don't you two go play in the hay.

Martin mounts the horse and rides into the center of the corral.

SUNSHINE
Stop it, Martin! Please! Stop!

The kids cheer as Martin rises to stand on the saddle. He loses his footing and falls and is dragged by the runaway horse, his ankle cracking in the stirrup.

DOCTOR'S OFFICE INTERIOR DAY

Jean and the doctor are examining the X-rays as they walk toward Martin in the emergency room.

DOCTOR
The only thing I can do is put him in a cast for a month or two and see how it mends.

JEAN
Is there anything further we can do?

DOCTOR
Not for him. But you better do something about her.

The doctor gestures to Barbara who is waiting outside Martin's room.

JEAN
Why?

DOCTOR
Well her father suspects she might be out here. He'll probably come out here with a search party tomorrow looking for her. Got any ideas?

JEAN
At the moment, I'm fresh out of them.

Barbara goes into Martin's room, smiles and silently hands him a flower. He smiles and takes it.

SCHOOL CAFETERIA INTERIOR DAY

The students are gathered as Jean silently reads a warrant handed to her by the Sheriff.

COLE
I want you to know that warrant isn't legal on reservation land, Jean. You don't have to let us search if you don't want to.

POSNER
Cole, whose side are you on? These people are holding this man's daughter illegally.

Jean looks at Posner, then goes up on the stage.

> **JEAN**
> *Hey, kids, they don't really have a right to search here, but if it'll make them feel like big men we're going to let them go ahead. Okay?*

As the police begin their search, Sarah goes up on the stage with her guitar.

> **ALL**
> *(singing)*
> *I was raised in Mississippi*
> *Sayin' yessir to the man*
> *But I found it got me nowhere*
> *So I won't say it again*
>
> *We're a rainbow made of children*
> *We're an army singing songs*
> *There's no weapon that can stop us*
> *Rainbow loving's much too strong*
>
> *They say they're christians*
> *They say they love him*
> *They say they love their golden rule*
> *Till they see it really working*
> *Like it is at Freedom School*
>
> *We're a rainbow, etc.*
>
> *I was taught that black is evil*
> *I was taught that white is good*
> *But when you become a rainbow*
> *Every color is understood*
>
> *We're a rainbow, etc. etc.*

As the police search the various areas of the school.

> **LYNN**
> *(singing)*

> *Big man Posner took his rifle*
> *Defending Mom and apple pie*
> *So I offered him a flower*
> *He just stood and he asked me why.*

Posner squirms in discomfort.

KIT
(singing)
My old grandma was a princess
And my granddad was a chief
Thanks to those of our white neighbors
Both my folks are on relief

ALL
(singing)
We're a rainbow, etc. etc.

What's important is the winning
And not how well you play the game
That's the way that Hitler saw it
And my folks, well, they see it the same

We're a rainbow made of children
We're an army singing songs
There's no weapon that can stop us
Rainbow loving's much too strong.

As the search continues without success, then . . .

COLE
Well one thing's pretty clear, Posner, she's not here.

POSNER
I guess that means Billy's taken her off. Don't you think you ought to find out where Billy is?

Cole walks away from the men across the room to Jean.

COLE
Jean, they want to know where Billy is.

47

JEAN
Who ever knows where Billy is?

COLE
Well you must have some way of getting in touch with him when you need him for emergencies.

JEAN
Whenever we want Billy we just contact him Indian style.

COLE
What does that mean?

JEAN
We just want him and somehow he shows up.

Mike has returned to Posner's side.

MIKE
How the hell are we going to find Billy on this reservation much less get Barbara away if we do?

COLE
Jean, this has gone far enough. I think we better find Barbara and forget the whole thing.

JEAN
(earnestly)
Cole, I honestly don't know where she is.

COLE
But if you did, you'd tell me.

JEAN
You know me better than that.

Posner realizes the Sheriff is not going to find Billy. He turns to Mike.

POSNER
The only way we're going to find Billy is we have to

> get one of these kids to tell us where he is. Offer
> them a reward, I'll back it up. A thousand dollars.

Bernard, overhearing, looks excitedly at his father.

BERNARD
One thousand dollars!

Mike goes up onstage, and tries to stop the students from
singing. They continue, and he shouts over their voices.

MIKE
*Kids, can I talk to you a minute? Can I talk to you
a minute, please?*
(they continue)
*Please, I want to talk to you. I want my daughter
back. She's sick. She needs help. She should be home
or in the hospital. Can't you damn kids listen? I'll
offer a thousand dollars. You can do it anony-
mously. Don't you darn kids know what you can do
with a thousand dollars? You can live in Big Sur for
a year. Damn hippie creeps.*

COLE
(aside, to Jean)
*Sorry I got you into all this, Jean. From now on it's
going to get very ugly, think about it for the sake of
all these kids, you think about it.*

JEAN
Will you tell?

COLE
Now you know me better than that.

They smile.

HILLTOP EXTERIOR DAY

Billy leads Barbara through a wood. Sunshine filters
through the brightly colored leaves as Billy pushes aside

low-hanging branches to open a path for Barbara. As they come to a clearing, Barbara sees a beautiful, vast expanse of ancient ruins. They climb a steep ladder into the heights of the ruins. Suddenly, Barbara is startled by the sight of Billy's old, deeply-wrinkled Indian teacher, sitting silently in a cave.

TOWN COUNCIL   INTERIOR   DAY

The council members sit at an elongated horseshoe-shaped table. Jean sits in the chamber which is filled with townspeople, students, and faculty members of the school.

CHAIRMAN
In view of the violence of the episode of the ice cream store, and in view of the extreme likelihood that only more such violence even more severe in nature is liable to erupt at any moment inflicting serious harm to members of the community as well as students and faculty at the school, and in the interest of everyone's safety and the establishment of law and order. The Board unanimously votes to request the city attorney to seek a court injunction restraining members of the Freedom School from coming into town except on Saturday between the hours of noon and four o'clock, and then only in groups of six or less. To the point of this resolution, we are now opening the floor, if you care to make a statement or ask a question affecting this matter.

PHIL
My name is Phil Crowder. I'm a student at the school . . . They beat him up, all those guys jumped Billy Jack, right?

DOCTOR
Mr. Chairman. . . .

CHAIRMAN
Will you yield?

PHIL
Sure.

DOCTOR
I'd like to remind this Board that the violence at the ice cream parlor was caused by the townspeople and that Billy Jack, the students from the school had nothing to do with it.

MARY
(glancing at the doctor)
Mr. Crowder, there is one man on our council here who agrees with you that it was not the fault of the school. . . .

DOCTOR
Wait a minute, well, Mary, there's a lot of citizens in this town who agree with me.

STUDENT
(shouting out)
Why don't you take a bath?

BOARD MEMBER
That's a beautiful statement.

CHAIRMAN
If you have something to say you will come forward and you will give your name and make your statement.

A teacher comes forward and addresses the council.

O.K.
O.K. Corrales.

CHAIRMAN
Respect this meeting enough to give your proper name.

O.K.
My proper name is O.K. Corrales. Do you have something against Mexicans?

CHAIRMAN
Let O.K. speak. O.K. wants to speak. Okay, O.K. do you have anything else to say, Mr. Corrales?

O.K.
To speak to the resolution, it opposes not only the spirit but the letter of the Constitution and many state and federal laws, and that's something you all ought to consider before you even bother sending it to the city attorney.

CHAIR
The chair recognizes Mr. Posner.

The students cheer and applaud.

STUDENT
But the door doesn't.

CHAIRMAN
(hammering)
The chair recognizes Mr. Posner.

POSNER
I respect what Mr. Corrales said. Our intentions are really parallel with his. We would like to preserve the peace. We would like to see the children unharmed and we are passing this measure with that intent. We would like not to have violence.

KIT
Then how come your son pours flour all over Indians.

The students cheer.

BOARD MEMBER
Mr. Johnson, when's the last time you cut your hair?

STUDENT
When's the last time you brushed your teeth, sir?

There is jeering from the chamber.

CHAIRMAN
(pounding gavel)
All right now, I want this meeting run orderly.

WOMAN BOARD MEMBER
Mr. Chairman, by our behavior as this council we're proving to these students that most of the things they believe about us are true, but they're proving to us that most of the things we fear about them are true.

YOUNG GIRL
Oh man, this council sucks.

Laughter.

Kit and Carol approach the front of the room.

CHAIRMAN
Proceed.

KIT
Yes, a little girl from the school has something she'd like to read.

CHAIRMAN
What's your name, young lady?

KIT
My name is Kit and her name is Carol and she has something she'd like to read.

BOARD MEMBER
How old are you, young lady?

CAROL
Eleven.

BOARD MEMBER
Eleven.

STUDENT
Too old for you.

POSNER
Just about old enough for you I guess, huh?

CHAIRMAN
Proceed young lady.

CAROL
(shyly at first)
I'd like to read a speech and after it's done I'd like you to guess who said it in public.
(she reads)
"The streets of our country are in turmoil, the universities are filled with students rebelling and rioting, Communists are seeking to destroy our country, Russia is threatening us with her might and the republic is in danger. Yes, danger from within and without. We need law and order. Without law and order our nation cannot survive." Who wrote it?

CHAIRMAN
Well, that's very nice, young lady.

KIT
You want to know who wrote it? Adolph Hitler wrote it in 1932 and everyone from Nixon's cabinet to your council is repeating it today.

POSNER
Now I'd like to know from this child if she would tell us who told her to read it here.

GIRL STUDENT
She has her own mind, she can read by herself you know.

POSNER
I wish she'd answer the question.

CAROL
Nobody told me to read it.

POSNER
Then why did you?

CAROL
I think I have a right to read what I want.

POSNER
Why did you read it?

BOARD MEMBER
Were you taught this in school?

ED
Because her brain is damaged by the heathen devil weed marijuana.

KIT
She still has the floor.

CAROL
I have another question for Mr. Posner. He ... this council here is always talking about law and order and things, well how come he kills stallions which is against the law?

BOARD MEMBER
This is irrelevant and immaterial.

GIRL STUDENT
I've been sitting here for over an hour and I've been listening to you and all I can see is that you're scared. I mean you're scared of all of us, you're scared of me and I don't know why you're scared of me.

55

BOARD MEMBER
We're scared of what you can do.

GIRL STUDENT
I'm going to come into town, but I'm not going to hurt you. I'm not going to do anything like that ... how do I intimidate you? Because, like I'm another human being. Are you scared of me sexually? What is it? I really want an answer.

BOARD MEMBER
I'll give you the answer. Because you're a filthy little girl.

Pandemonium breaks out in the chamber. There is an explosion of argument and shouting. Some of the students throw paper gliders toward the council members, as another plays "The Star Spangled Banner" on a saxophone.

CHAIRMAN
(shouting over the din)
Order! You are out of order. If you want to speak, you will have your opportunity.

O.K.
Hold it! Hold it! Everybody's a little crazy.

WOMAN BOARD MEMBER
And you people think you're free.

O.K.
Why don't we all just calm down, probably the best thing to do would be if you all could come out to the school and see what we do in our natural habitat.

BOARD MEMBER
This is a fine example of what you do. We have invited you to this council. . . .

STUDENT
. . . and we have invited you to our school.

JEAN
*Sir, Chairman, this is no more an example of what
the school is like than it is for what the town is like
and what you're like as people.*

BOARD MEMBER
*It is not important what the school is like; it is what
you are going to do in this town. This is the example.*

JEAN
Are you afraid? Come out to the school and see us.

WOMAN BOARD MEMBER
Yes, I for one am afraid.

JEAN
Will any of you come to the school?

CHAIRMAN
Very well, very well. I will come to your school.

SCHOOL   INTERIOR   DAY

The auditorium is packed with people watching two students seated in two chairs, driving an imginary car, doing
a role-playing scene. Howard is at the wheel, obviously
"stoned."

HOWARD
*I don't know man, I don't really feel loaded, you
know. We should smoke another one.*

ED
Okay, my grass or yours?

HOWARD
They all taste the same past a certain point.

ED
Oh yeah? I think your taste buds have burned out.

Ed lights an imaginary joint.

HOWARD
*No, actually it's my brain that's burned out. Better
cool it, there's a plainclothes car coming at the inter-
section.*

Ed ducks below the seat. Howard pulls him back up.

HOWARD
*Come on, man, straighten up and act normal. You
sure look wierd when you're acting normal. The red
ones mean stop, right?*

Ed passes Howard the imaginary joint.

ED
Right.

Howard steps on the "brakes." Ed flies forward into the
dash board. Howard grins, trying to pretend he knew what
he was doing.

HOWARD
Keeps you on your toes.

ED
*Don't you think you better pull up to the intersec-
tion?*

HOWARD
(caught not in control of himself)
Just testing you.

ED
*Hey, look over in the next car, a couple of high
school kids passing a joint around. I'll turn on the
red light.*

HOWARD
(in his authoritative "cop" voice)

Right. You kids want to pull over up here?

There is laughter and applause from the students. Two members of the town council, Mr. Eldridge, the Chairman, and Mrs. Osgood are also watching.

O.K.
What did you think of it?

MRS. OSGOOD
I don't know. It seems a little one-sided.

HOWARD
But kids look at things one-sided. Most of the things they're looking at are one-sided.

O.K.
Let's try something. By the way, does everybody know Mr. Eldridge and Mrs. Osgood from the council?

The kids applaud as they are introduced.

O.K.
Why don't we do another scene which involves policemen and differing attitudes, and we can use your attitudes as well as ours. Kit, why don't you come up too?

Kit comes up and introduces herself.

O.K.
Why don't ... Kit, you be the mother and Howard you be a father, a family together. And Ed, why don't you be the Sheriff ... Cole. And the two of you will be teen-age children of this family.

MRS. OSGOOD
I just can't.

O.K.
Sure!

MRS. OSGOOD
I just can't do that.

O.K.
Okay, Sheriff, why don't you arrest them for marihuana, and then bring them home to their parents and explain the situation.

MR. ELDRIDGE
(trying to be "with it")
Ready to be busted?

O.K. leaves the stage and they all take their positions. Ed then takes Mrs. Osgood and Mr. Eldridge by their arms over to the make-believe front door.

ED
You're under arrest. Come with me. Hello Kit, what brings me here is these two.

HOWARD
Some trouble, Sheriff?

ED
Yes, Howard, I'm very sorry to have to come here for this but these children have been smoking marihuana with a known dope fiend.

KIT
What?

ED
Marihuana.

KIT
(wailing)
Our children. Oh, no!

HOWARD
All right now, just be calm. I want to thank you again for coming down.

ED
I'm sorry.

HOWARD
That's all right. See you Saturday night at the tennis matches!

ED
(leaving)
Bye, Kit. Love from Marge.

HOWARD
(to hysterical Kit)
Just calm down.

KIT
How can I calm down at a time like this?

HOWARD
Sit down.

KIT
How can I sit down?

HOWARD
Bend your legs and sit.

Kit does as she's told.

HOWARD
Calm down. Okay, what happened?

MR. ELDRIDGE
Nothing happened. Can you believe me? Nothing happened.

HOWARD
He lied to us? Listen we pay that man to tell us the truth. Now what happened?

MR. ELDRIDGE
Nothing happened.

HOWARD
You owe me an honest explanation. I want to hear it right now.

MR. ELDRIDGE
(bowing on his hands and knees to Howard)
I'm not your dog.

HOWARD
Are you high on the stuff? Get up.

MR. ELDRIDGE
Don't yell at me.

KIT
What happened?

MRS. OSGOOD
Nothing. Nothing happened.

HOWARD
Were you smoking this dope or not?

He threatens to hit Mr. Eldridge.

MRS. OSGOOD
Violent creature.

A knock is heard at the imaginary door.

HOWARD
Get the door, Kit.

She doesn't move. She is too hysterical.

HOWARD
Get the door. Tell them we don't want any.
(to Mrs. Osgood)
Watch television, watch the television and enjoy it.

Barbara (JULIE WEBB), pregnant unwed daughter of Wallich's deputy sheriff, is accepted in a ceremony by the others at the Freedom School after she runs away from home following a beating by her outraged father. The school agrees to hide her.

Half-breed Billy Jack (TOM LAUGHLIN) defends Jean Roberts' (DELORES TAYLOR) Freedom School for troubled young-adults on an Indian Reservation from the violent opposition of residents of the neighboring town of Wallich.

Billy Jack is initiated into Shoshone "manhood" by enduring repeated rattler bites. While recovering alone he is unaware that Barbara has been thrown from a horse, losing her baby. Bernard, son of a prominent townsman, spreads the lie that Barbara is "secing" a young Indian.

THE ODDS ARE AGAINST HIM, but Tom Laughlin prepares to defend himself by the use of hapkido, a form of karate, in this scene from "Billy Jack," the new Warner Bros. release starring Laughlin and Delores Taylor. Contemporary drama was directed by T. C. Frank and produced by Mary Rose Solti.

Learning of the rape and murder, Billy Jack corners Bernard and, after taking a bullet in the side, kills Bernard with a karate chop to the throat. The town mounts a posse and corners Billy Jack in a deserted bunkhouse.

Opposite: After a bloody siege, Billy Jack agrees to surrender for trial, to Sheriff Cole (CLARK HOWAT) and deputies, in exchange for guarantees that Jean be allowed to run her school without interference and that she be given custody of Barbara.

MRS. OSGOOD
(clapping her hands)
Ha ha! Ha Ha! Ha!

Cindy and Ray, playing neighbors, enter the scene.

CINDY
I wondered if everything was all right.

HOWARD
Their car broke down and Sheriff Cole was kind enough to bring them home.

Outraged at this phony story, Mr. Eldridge turns.

MR. ELDRIDGE
You hypocrite.

HOWARD
You watch your language, young man.

MR. ELDRIDGE
You told me. . . .

HOWARD
Never mind what I told you, I'm telling you something different now.

MR. ELDRIDGE
Oh, it's a whole new set of lies.

HOWARD
Show some respect for your father. Sit down or I'll thrash you.

Jean, Sheriff Cole and the Doctor. They are laughing uproariously at the marvelous way the whole role-playing technique is working.

SCHOOL INTERIOR DAY

The audience is leaving the gymnasium.

MR. ELDRIDGE
If you ask me, I think you ought to put on a whole show, invite the whole town out here, let them know what you're doing up here.

JEAN
Why not?

HILLTOP   EXTERIOR   DAY

Barbara is sitting high up on a ledge among the ruins as Jean approaches on horseback and calls up to her.

JEAN
Is Billy still in the kiva?

BARBARA
No. Some braves came and took him away.

JEAN
Would you like to come watch the ceremony with me?

BARBARA
(excitedly)
Would I?

She comes down and mounts the horse behind Jean. They start to ride to a viewpoint from which they can watch the ceremony. They join the group assembled to witness Billy's initiation.

BARBARA
What is the snake ceremony?

JEAN
It's a ceremony where Billy becomes a brother to the snake.

BARBARA
How does he do that?

JEAN
(v.o.)
*By going on the mountain and being bitten by a
snake over and over. Then he passes into uncon-
sciousness for the last time, and, if he lives, he has a
vision, and in this vision he finds out what his life's
mission will be and who the spirit will be to guide
him on this mission.*

KIVA ENTRANCE EXTERIOR DAY

Down in the pit of an old kiva, sacred Indian dances are
being performed by the leading members of the tribe. In
the center, four drummers are beating a drum and chanting simultaneously. The air is heavy with some sort of
expectation.

Jean and Barbara enter past an Indian chief in full war
bonnet and take their place next to Kit and Martin and
Carol.

A brave pulls aside a sacred blanket and Billy Jack, in full
ceremonial costume—white buckskin warrior's dress beau-
tifully beaded and fringed, his face painted with ceremonial paint—moves to the center holding an eagle feather.

And also during this purification part, Billy is given a
secret herb medicine and then given a sacred poultice to
put on the bites . . .

The Indians, in full ceremonial costume, led by the drummers, are leading Billy Jack, who is on horseback. They
are going up the mountain to the place where the snake
ceremony will take place.

SACRED GROUNDS EXTERIOR DAY

JEAN
. . . without it he would die for sure. It takes about

three days for the poison to work its way through his body, and by then it will either kill him or make him a blood brother to the snake.

Oh, listen, the old man is giving him the final blessing.

OLD MAN
(v.o.)
Achiva the snake waits for you upon sacred mountain. If you pass this test, then you will have a vision. It is not easy and if you show fear you shall die. Hold onto this eagle feather and do not let it go, regardless of what you see or what you hear. The demons will come and try to scare you, but show no fear or you shall die. May the great spirit watch over you.

Billy, holding the feather and a pouch of sacred powder, sits cross-legged, alone in the pit with the rattlesnake. He rises and dances around the snake, sprinkling the ground with sacred powder as he moves. The snake strikes at Billy's leg. Billy flinches, but continues his dance.

The snake strikes repeatedly, each time finding its mark. Billy drops to his knees, grabs the snake and pulls it from his leg. It slithers away as Billy slumps to the ground, his face in the dust. Billy weakly resumes his sitting, cross-legged position, but is overcome and falls on his side, unconscious, the feather and pouch still in his hand.

RUINS EXTERIOR DAY

Barbara Jean, Carol, and Kit wait in the old ruins as night falls. There is still no word from Billy as the Indians continue chanting below.

BARBARA
How long before we know?

JEAN
Tomorrow.

HILLTOP EXTERIOR DAY

The sun rises. Billy Jack lifts his arms to salute it. He has become a brother to the snake.

KIVA EXTERIOR DAY

Billy has been brought back to the kiva and is addressing the tribe.

MOUNTAIN TOP EXTERIOR DAY

Bernard has Billy in a close-up in the scope of his high-powered rifle.

KIVA EXTERIOR DAY

BILLY
The time is now when the Indian will triumpn.

JEAN
(quietly, to Barbara)
He's still in the rapture of the vision. A great Indian holy man, Wovoka, is speaking through him.

BARBARA
You mean they had holy men like saints?

JEAN
They sure did, and Wovoka was one of the greatest. Once even Christ appeared to him.

BILLY
The whole spiritual wisdom of the great holy men, the Indian tradition is now what the young people of the world are looking for.

MOUNTAIN TOP EXTERIOR DAY

Bernard is holding Billy in his sights.

BERNARD
I wonder if I have the guts.

DINOSAUR
This is crazy, man. You pull that trigger and we'll never get out of here alive.

KIVA EXTERIOR DAY

BILLY
The young whites, they know there is a supernatural world and a Great Spirit and they try to reach the Great Spirit. They try by drugs. They are made to do this because their religions no longer believe in the other world. Heaven is not out there. The other world is here. The Great Spirit, Messiah, Christ, are here in this pit. Your people, my loved ones. There is a thin veil separating us from them. The whites do not know how to reach through that veil. They do not have the belief and they cannot touch their loved ones or the other spirits.

MOUNTAIN TOP EXTERIOR DAY

Slowly Bernard squeezes the trigger. Click. He did not have a shell in the gun.

BERNARD
I could do it. I could kill him.

DINOSAUR
Yeah, sure you can, but not now, man. Let's get out of here and get some help.

KIVA EXTERIOR DAY

BILLY
And lastly you must learn the dance, the dance of friendship and welcome in which all whites who come to you with open hearts must be taught to dance in the Indian way. Rise up now and I will

teach you the dance exactly as Wovoka has shown it shall be done.

The Indians rise and start taking positions.

MOUNTAIN TOP EXTERIOR DAY

> **BERNARD**
> *Yeah, we will be back but not with help. I'm going to get him all by myself.*

> **DINOSAUR**
> *Hey, Bernard, isn't that Barbara?*

Through his binoculars, Dinosaur sees Barbara and Martin walking and laughing together down by the lake.

> **BERNARD**
> *Goddamn! She's really screwing around with an Indian. I thought that was just talk.*

Bernard takes a picture of Martin and Barbara.

KIVA EXTERIOR DAY

Below them, the Indians dance the dance from Billy's vision. As they coil in a long rhythmically moving line around Billy, he obviously is in a trance.

TOWN EXTERIOR DAY

Jean, Kit, Cindy, and Martin pull up in front of the paint store in the jeep.

> **JEAN**
> *Okay, Martin, you run in and get the paint and we'll pick you up later. Okay?*

> **MARTIN**
> *(struggling on his crutches)*
> *Okay. How do you expect me to carry all the paint?*

CINDY
(laughing)
Oh, you hang it from the top of your crutches.

From inside the paint store, Bernard and Dinosaur see Martin outside.

DINOSAUR
Lookee here!

Bernard comes over and sees Martin in here alone.

STORE INTERIOR DAY

Jean, Kit, and Cindy are buying clothes for Barbara's baby.

JEAN
Can we bring it back in case it's a boy?

KIT
(holding Indian baby boots)
Look at these.

They squeal with delight.

PAINT STORE INTERIOR DAY

Deputy Mike, Bernard, and Dinosaur have got Martin cornered in a back room.

MIKE
And if you help us get her out of there, you'll not only collect that big fat reward I offered but you'll save someone's life.

MARTIN
Like whose?

MIKE
Yours.

70

BERNARD
And Billy Jack's.

Mike presses a lead pipe against Martin's throat.

MIKE
But if you fail to help us, as sure as this pipe is at your throat you're going to be one hell of a dead Indian. Savvy?

BERNARD
(firing Mike's fury)
You know, I think he's sweet on her. Didn't it look that way to you, Dinosaur?

DINOSAUR
Yeah.

BERNARD
Holding hands, kissing her.

Mike hits Martin in the stomach with the lead pipe. Martin doubles over in pain.

PAINT STORE   EXTERIOR   DAY

Jean, Kit, and Cindy pull up outside in the jeep. They notice the Sheriff's car and become alarmed.

PAINT STORE   INTERIOR   DAY

Martin is on the floor gasping for breath.

MIKE
Now you listen to me, grease ball, if you ever touch her again, I'm going to cripple your other leg, and I don't mean the one you walk on, hear?

The girls charge in and Jean rushes to help Martin.

JEAN
What the hell do you think you're doing?

Mike gets up and tries to act very cordial.

> **MIKE**
> *Oh, I guess the boys found him sneaking out the back without paying. Right, Sam?*

He looks over to the frightened store owner. Jean glares at him.

> **SAM**
> *Uh . . . yeah, that's right.*

> **JEAN**
> *What are the charges then, Sam?*

Sam doesn't answer. She turns to Mike.

> **JEAN**
> *You heard me, what are the charges?*

Jean helps Martin up from the floor.

> **MIKE**
> *Charges? Well, no charges. Sam here is a pretty good guy. You're not going to press charges are you Sam?*

Again Jean whirls to glare at Sam. He is badly frightened by Mike.

> **SAM**
> *No charges.*

> **JEAN**
> *(bitterly)*
> *No, you're a nice guy, aren't you, Sam.*

Jean takes Martin and Cindy starts to come at Mike.

> **CINDY**
> *You're a dirty, rotten, lying . . .*

Kit grabs her arm and spins her around to avoid her hitting Mike but finishes her line.

KIT
. . . son of a bitch!

SCHOOL   INTERIOR   DAY

The improvisational group, sitting on a stage, is debating what to do.

O.K.
Because of the injunction we're going to do it by their rules but we're going to do it with our attitudes. And what we want to do—we're going to send six people, because that's as much as we can, into town and we're going to do some street theater.

CAROL
Sure, why let Bernard and the Deputy ruin all the friendships we're starting to build.

STUDENT
It just pulls us down to their level.

TOWN SQUARE   EXTERIOR   DAY

One of the students, dressed as a businessman, wearing a hat and carrying a briefcase, is on the corner waiting for the bus. Howard approaches him, looks around, and pulls out a gun, placing it surreptitiously in his back.

HOWARD
Okay! Give me your money! Come on!

DONALD
Uh . . . I left my wallet at home.

HOWARD
Got any change?

DONALD
Sorry.

HOWARD
What's in the briefcase?

DONALD
Yogurt.

HOWARD
Got a wrist watch?

DONALD
Well, it's a Timex.

HOWARD
What did you pay for the band?

Ed is sitting nearby on a park bench, and gets up to interrupt.

ED
No man, it doesn't work. That doesn't scare me. You've blown it as a robber.

Howard, the robber, is stunned at this casual intrusion.

ED
You've got to come out here and give this man something for his trouble. I as a spectator felt nothing for you other than total embarrassment.

HOWARD
Oh—well, sorry!

ED
No. That's not enough. You've got to let this man know that as a robber you are going to give a performance to the robbee. You've got no energy. In theater it's a place where you get your energy from the center, see, so that you just bring it out all at

once. Now, what's the first emotion that comes into
your head?

HOWARD
Oh! Well—uh . . . confusion.

ED
*All right, then, use that. Bring out that energy. Do
you have any bullets in the gun?*

HOWARD
No, I didn't want to hurt anybody.

ED
*Oh well, you see! You should put a bullet in there so
that he knows. See? Or at least make him think
there are bullets in there. Did you think there were
any bullets in the gun?*

DONALD
Well, I wasn't very intimidated.

HOWARD
Sorry.

ED
*Okay, well it doesn't work that way. You take the
gun and you put a bullet in it and you have this feeling of power that you plant in the back of your
brain. And you mix it with your energy so that when
you come out, you come out a dynamo of robbery,
a man who's going to get respect as well as money.*
(he turns to Donald)
*I'm going to be robbing you in just a second, so hold
on.*
(back to Howard)
*I'm going to show you exactly what I mean. You've
got yourself together as a robber and you can't even
keep it down because it's all flowing out so fast.
Keep it cool and you play it yourself and this man
won't know what's happening.*

He takes the gun and slowly approaches Donald with the hidden gun.

ED
You come up to him very cool. "Let's have your money." Let's go.

He places the gun at Donald's head as Sheriff Cole approaches the group from behind.

COLE
Freeze! I don't want to hurt you, son, so don't you make any sudden moves. Now, you just very slowly drop that gun down on the sidewalk. Put your hands up above your head.

Ed drops the gun and does as he is told. Howard, who is on the curb, turns his back on the group on the sidewalk and puts out his thumb to hitch hike.

COLE
Move to your right. Keep moving.
(turning away from Ed to see Howard trying to sneak off)
Hey you!

Ed drops his hands and berates Cole.

ED
No, man, no. Absolutely not. You took your eyes off of me and I'm the suspect. And you look at me and you get me and you don't say freeze while I've got a gun pointed at his head. I could freeze his brains out. There's an honest tax paying citizen ready to blow his own foot off because you haven't put the situation in your control.

Donald lifts the gun away from his foot.

ED
Something short and sharp and authoritative like "Drop the gun and up against the wall."

Donald drops the gun.

> **HOWARD**
> *Hey! Watch it. That's a new gun.*

Jean, Kit, and Cissy are among the crowd that is watching.

> **COLE**
> *What's going on here?*

> **DONALD**
> *I think it would be a lot clearer if perhaps we just simply did it all over again.*

> **ED**
> *Good idea. Here's your gun. Remember, energy is what's important.*

> **DONALD**
> *I'm waiting for the bus, right?*

> **COLE**
> *What have I got here, three psychos?*

> **DONALD**
> *You're not even here yet.*

> **COLE**
> *(puzzled)*
> *Oh! Sorry.*

He walks away in the direction from which he came.

> **HOWARD**
> *Give me your money because I'm confused and I'm liable to explode at any minute.*

Cole comes in, pulls out his gun, stammers, and then lowers his arms.

COLE
I forgot the line.

ED
"Drop the gun and up against the wall."

COLE
I can't drop the gun, I've got bullets in it.

ED
Well, then take the bullets out.

Cole does so.

DONALD
(to Cole)
I've got an idea. You take the briefcase. All right now, look. You stand over here. Let's do the whole thing from the beginning. You're a businessman. . . .

Donald and Cole exchange hats.

ED
Let him discover all that for himself.

DONALD
All right, good idea.

Cole, ridiculous in the smaller hat, takes his place by the bus stop.

COLE
What if the bus comes, do I get on it?

ED
Don't play it that real.

HOWARD
Okay, give me all your money right now or I have bad news.

DONALD
(trying to aim his gun at Howard over Cole's head)
All right, drop the gun.

ED
I think that gesture is a little too flamboyant, I wouldn't use that. But you get the tone.

DONALD
Right. The line was right!

ED
Let's take it from the top once more please. You're beginning to mesh as a unit.

DONALD
Can I be the robber this time?

ED
Sure, mix it up.

COLE
Can I have my hat?

DONALD
Didn't I do it right that time?

ED
No, everything's fine, he just wants to play another part.

COLE
I get to be the Sheriff, but I'm not here yet.

ED
No, you're not here.

Cole turns obediently away to await his cue.

HOWARD
(to Donald)

> *I'm warning you, if you drop the gun again, I'm going to mess up the briefcase. Now I'm waiting for the bus. Where is that darn bus? Madge and the kids are going. . . .*

Cole comes in and forgets his line again.

ED
You've got to be prepared.

COLE
All right, one of you, I don't care who it is, get up there and drop the gun.

Donald drops the gun again on the sidewalk and Howard slams down the briefcase.

HOWARD
I warned you if you dropped the gun. . . .

They break out in fake bedlam.

COLE
(smiling in the direction of the crowd)
Okay, Jean, is that enough?

DONALD
You knew she was there?

COLE
I knew she was there, you knew she was there. We all knew. Jean was out there all the time.

ED
Come by the school anytime.

All the townspeople who had been watching the scene, crowd around the students. At the edge of the square, Cissie gets in Bernard's Corvette and they drive away. Kit watches them go.

LAKESIDE EXTERIOR DAY

Cissie and Bernard sit in Bernard's Corvette. Cissie is agog at such an expensive car.

> **BERNARD**
> *You like nice things, don't you?*

> **CISSIE**
> *You better believe it.*

> **BERNARD**
> *(taking Cissie's hand)*
> *Maybe you can have them sooner than you think.*

> **CISSIE**
> *Just what's that supposed to mean?*

> **BERNARD**
> *You heard the Deputy. He'll pay a thousand dollars just to find out where his daughter is, no questions asked.*

> **CISSIE**
> *Look, those kids are my friends. What kind of a person do you think I am?*

> **BERNARD**
> *One who would do anything for a buck.*

Cissie tries to slap Bernard, who wards off the blow. He reaches into the glove compartment, pulls out a knife and clicks it open in front of her.

> **BERNARD**
> *Where's Billy Jack hiding Barbara?*

> **CISSIE**
> *I honestly don't know.*

BERNARD
*Okay Miss False Eyelashes, off with your blouse.
Off!*

Cissie, frightened, hurriedly pulls her blouse over her
head.

BERNARD
Where's Barbara?

CISSIE
*Please, please. I don't know where she is. None of
the kids do. I'd tell you if I knew, I would. But I
don't know where she is.*

Bernard cuts the front of her bra.

BERNARD
All the way off.

Suddenly, Jean drives up in her jeep and Billy Jack follows
her on his motorcycle. For a long time no one knows
what to say. Then, surprisingly, Billy starts to chuckle.

BILLY
I can't believe it. I really can't believe this guy.
(to Jean)
Can you believe it?

JEAN
(chuckling at Bernard's asininity)
Not really, no.

BILLY
You know what he reminds me of?

JEAN
What?

BILLY
A monkey. Posner's little monkey ... running

around trying to get in all the bananas.
(to Cissie)
Get your blouse and get out of here.

CISSIE
Will you look?

BILLY
Probably! Go on and get your blouse.

Cissie retrieves her clothes, and jumps into the jeep beside Jean.

BILLY
Okay, Bernard, get out of the car and let's teach you a lesson that your daddy should have taught you a long time ago.

JEAN
No, Billy, you can't do it. If you hurt Bernard they're going to close down the school and ruin everything we've tried to build.

BILLY
What do you suggest I do?

JEAN
Teach him a lesson but without really hurting him.

BILLY
How?

Jean is groping for something to stop Billy's anger.

JEAN
Why don't you drive his car into the lake?

Bernard whirls and looks at Jean.

BILLY
What?

JEAN
I said why don't you drive his car into the lake?

Bernard snaps his head to Billy to see if he is buying it.

BILLY
(grinning)
You know, that's not a bad thought for a pacifist.

JEAN
(laughing) -
We have our days.

BILLY
(laughing)
All right, Bernard. Which is it going to be? Drive your car into the lake or get a dislocated elbow?

BERNARD
What do you mean broken elbow? What are you nuts or something?

BILLY
Yeah, a lot of people think so. But then we're stuck with that, you and I. Now which is it going to be?

BERNARD
Hey, my old man's gonna kill me if anything happens. You know he just bought this car for me. I mean he'll kill me if I hurt this car really.

Billy gets off the motorcycle and crosses to the car. He stands over Bernard.

BILLY
Oh come on, Bernard, you get to choose. Which is it gonna be?

BERNARD
What if I drive away? Or take the knife?

BILLY
Bernard I wish you would. I really wish you would.

JEAN
Don't, Bernard. You don't stand a chance.

Bernard glares at Jean.

BERNARD
Next time I'll cut off your bra.

BILLY
Now you gotta choose.

Billy turns on the ignition.

BILLY
When I count to three, you drive your car in the lake. One . . . two . . . floor it!

Bernard drives the car into the lake and, as it sinks, he swims out.

LAKESIDE EXTERIOR DAY

Bernard sits wet and shivering in a blanket. Across the lake a tow truck is parked, having just pulled Bernard's car from the water.

A furious Posner is confronting Bernard.

POSNER
You're going to sit there and tell me that he didn't pull a gun on you, a knife—nothing!

BERNARD
Nothing.

POSNER
He just told you to drive the car into the lake and you obeyed him. Why didn't you drive away?

BERNARD
I was scared.

POSNER
You were what?

BERNARD
(screaming)
I was scared!

POSNER
You were scared. You were scared! So you drove a six thousand dollar automobile into the lake. Why you're nothing but a lousy coward!

He slaps Bernard in the face and storms off. Then he walks to Cole.

POSNER
Cole, things are getting uglier and uglier around here. There's nothing but a lot of hotheads in town who would like nothing better than to charge right up to that school now and start a fire. Unless you do something, there's going to be a lot of innocent people on both sides getting hurt.

COLE
Suppose we begin by pressing charges.

POSNER
What kind of charges? What can we prove? That my son's an idiot. A stupid coward, what else?

COLE
I told you, Stuart, I'll handle it.

BARN EXTERIOR DAY

Jean has saddled a horse for an afternoon ride when Barbara opens the gate for her.

JEAN
How come you're hanging around down here, Bar-
bara?
(teasingly)
It wouldn't have anything to do with Martin, would
it?

They glance at Martin loading hay.

BARBARA
Martin?

JEAN
Listen, I'm going to go for a swim, but you stay off
that horse now, you hear?

BARBARA
Yes, momma.

Jean rides off toward the mountains.

BARN   INTERIOR   DAY

Martin is stacking bales of hay as Barbara sits among
them, watching him work.

BARBARA
How come you never tried to lay me?

MARTIN
That's a stupid question.

BARBARA
Don't cover up, are you afraid of me?

MARTIN
No, I'm not afraid.

BARBARA
Then what? Wasn't I good enough for you? I heard
all Indian boys want to go to bed with white girls.

MARTIN
Don't believe everything you hear.

BARBARA
But I know you want to, I can tell. How come you never tried?

Martin thinks a moment, then,

MARTIN
Because you've always been an anybody's.

BARBARA
What's an anybody's?

MARTIN
An anybody's is someone who puts out so she can get dates and be accepted. I want you to experience the fact that I don't love you because you'll give me some sex. I love you for yourself and what you are. You see, you're a very soft and beautiful person and I love you very much.

Martin takes out his wallet and removes a piece of paper, which he hands to Barbara. She studies it a moment, then looks up.

BARBARA
(puzzled)
What's this?

MARTIN
A saying by Saint Francis of Assisi. It's kind of dumb but go ahead and read it.

BARBARA
"Lord grant me the serenity to accept the things I cannot change, and courage to change the things I can and the wisdom to know the difference."

MARTIN
My mother left that to me, it was all she had.

Moved, Barbara tries to hand the paper back to Martin, but he doesn't take it.

    MARTIN
    I want you to have it.

MOUNTAIN EXTERIOR DAY

His arm hooked under his rifle, Dinosaur is looking across the valley through a set of binoculars.

    BERNARD
    Tell me, Dinosaur, why is it, when a guy hates his old man as much as I do, he'll still keep trying to do that one thing that he'll be proud of?

    DINOSAUR
    What makes you think Billy's going to be by here. I mean, he could be in Africa for all we know. My God, Bernard, hey. . . .

LAKESIDE EXTERIOR DAY

Dinosaur has Jean in close-up through the sights of his binoculars. She is getting undressed beside the lake.

MOUNTAIN EXTERIOR DAY

    BERNARD
    What?

    DINOSAUR
    Look at that.

Bernard takes the binoculars and raises them to his eyes.

LAKESIDE EXTERIOR DAY

Jean is in close-up through the sights of the binoculars. She is swimming in the nude.

BERNARD
(v.o.)
Goddamn.

MOUNTAIN EXTERIOR DAY

DINOSAUR
What are we going to do now?

LAKESIDE EXTERIOR DAY

Jean is lying in the grass, dozing peacefully under the hot sun, nude. Bernard approaches stealthily and presses the rifle into her throat. Jean opens her eyes.

BERNARD
One move, one sound, one twitch of your eyelash and you are dead.

CORRAL EXTERIOR DAY

Barbara is riding a horse at a full gallop. Martin watches uneasily.

MARTIN
Put your feet forward! Hang onto the horn!

As the horse races, it sweeps into a roll of tumbleweed and rears, throwing Barbara. She hits the ground hard.

LAKESIDE EXTERIOR DAY

Jean is tied down, the ropes tight, almost drawing blood. Bernard is sitting, and says to no one in particular:

BERNARD
(casually)
You know, for all my bragging, I've never really been able to go all the way with a girl. Every time I get worked up, I can't finish it.

Bernard gets up and bends over Jean, putting a hand on her body. Jean tries to twist away.

BERNARD
If it was so funny when my car went into the lake, how come you're not laughing now?

DOCTOR'S OFFICE   INTERIOR   DAY

Barbara is in the hospital bed.

DOCTOR
Martin, have you found Jean yet?

MARTIN
We've sent for her.

DOCTOR
You better hurry up. I'm afraid Barbara's going to lose that baby.

LAKESIDE   EXTERIOR   DAY

Bernard is running his hand along Jean's thigh.

JEAN
Bernard, this is kidnap and rape. You stop now and I'll forget it. You go on and I swear I'll see you in prison for the rest of your life.

BERNARD
Not a chance. You got no witnesses. Whose word do you think my old man and the Sheriff will believe anyway—yours or ours?

Bernard lowers himself over Jean and tries to kiss her. Jean bites his lip savagely. He pulls back and touches the blood seeping from his lip.

BERNARD
You lousy rotten bitch.

JEAN
You touch me again and I'll scream.

Dinosaur looks around, worried. Bernard lifts the gun and drops the muzzle against Jean's face.

BERNARD
You let out one sound and I'll put a bullet right in your mouth.

JEAN
Then you better pull the trigger right now because I would rather die than have you touch me again.

Jean lets out a long, loud scream and pulls against the ropes. Bernard and Dinosaur move to gag her.

OPEN RANGE EXTERIOR DAY

Kit and Cindy, riding easily, hear the scream.

KIT
(reining in)
Try Peer Lake.

They wheel their mounts and dig hard in separate directions.

LAKESIDE EXTERIOR DAY

BERNARD
You know part of me doesn't really want to do this.

DINOSAUR
Then let's get out of here.

Slowly, Bernard climbs on Jean. Dinosaur looks around, then hurriedly snugs Jean's head between his hands and holds her in a tighter grip.

LAKE EXTERIOR DAY

Cindy, cantering through the lakeside pines, pulls her mount up sharply. Through the trees she sees Bernard and Dinosaur. Cindy digs her heels into the horse's flanks and urges it into a wild run.

LAKESIDE EXTERIOR DAY

Cindy breaks from the stand of pine.

> **CINDY**
> *Billy! Kit! They're down here! Help! Billy!*

Bernard and Dinosaur look up.

> **BERNARD**
> *Christ, man, let's get out of here.*

Bernard grabs his rifle and he and Dinosaur run toward their car.

Cindy rides up, dismounts, and runs to Jean. Crying uncontrollably, Cindy unties the ropes.

LAKESIDE EXTERIOR DAY

Jean is dressed and she and Cindy are sitting near the lake. Neither has said anything. Jean continues to look across the lake. Cindy seems less able than Jean to bear her pain.

> **CINDY**
> *(softly)*
> *I pray that Billy kills him.*

> **JEAN**
> *You mustn't tell Billy, Cindy.*

> **CINDY**
> *Why not?*

> **JEAN**
> *Because he will kill him.*

CINDY
(angrily)
Damn your pacifism! I am not going to let that sick animal get away with this.

JEAN
He has gotten away with it. Even if Billy kills him, kills them all, it wouldn't change what's happened here today. It wouldn't take away any of the horror. It would just destroy a lot of innocent kids, can't you understand that?

Cindy stares straight ahead, unconvinced.

JEAN
My religion, my nonviolence, the kids, that's all I have left now. If you rob me of this chance, if I can't really turn the other cheek when I can help the kids the most, then I couldn't endure what happened here today. If they took the school away, I just couldn't live with what happened here. Please, Cindy, please.

DOCTOR'S OFFICE   INTERIOR   DAY

Billy Jack, Jean, Cindy, and some of the students are in the corridor waiting to hear about Barbara. Billy moves to Jean's side.

BILLY
Hey, what happened?

JEAN
I guess she got thrown when she was trying to do some trick riding.

Billy sees Cindy looking at Jean strangely. Billy looks closely at Jean.

BILLY
What else is wrong? Come on, I've never see you act so strange.

JEAN
I guess I'm just upset about Barbara.

Cindy and Jean exchange glances. Billy studies Cindy, who quickly looks away. The doctor comes out of the operating room.

DOCTOR
It was a boy, white. We lost him.

MOUNTAIN   EXTERIOR   DAY

A long single-file line of students works its way along the steep mountain path. A log ladder spills the students into an old Indian ruin on a narrow ledge.

Raised high on four poles is a platform, on which Barbara's dead baby, wrapped in furs, has been placed.

Barbara takes her place beside the funeral pyre.

The song that opens the scene continues:

GIRL
(singing, v. o.)
Mary had a little baby
Born in Bethlehem
Every time the little baby cried
She rocked him with a weary hand
Ain't that rotten for the world
Ain't that rotten for the world
Ain't that rotten for the world
Oh she rocked him with a weary hand.

SCHOOL PORCH   EXTERIOR   DAY

Billy stands leaning against a post. Martin sits nearby.

BILLY
Martin, do you know what mental toughness is?
Well, mental toughness is the ability to accept the

*fact that you're human and you're going to make
mistakes, lots of them, all your life. Some of them
are going to hurt people, that you love, very badly,
but you have the guts to accept the fact that you're
imperfect and you don't let your mistakes crush you
and keep you from trying to do the very best that
you can.*

MARTIN
A lot of good I could've done.

BILLY
You sure could've.
(Martin turns questioningly to Billy)
*You could've gone inside and comforted that girl in-
stead of sitting out here on the porch whining and
feeling so sorry for yourself.*

Billy steps off the porch and walks away.

BARBERSHOP INTERIOR DAY

Several men are lounging about. The doctor sits in the
barber's chair, having his hair cut.

MIKE
*The only reason they cremated it was to keep us
from knowing it was that Indian's kid.*

DOCTOR
*It was not an Indian, I told you. I handled it, it was
a white fetus.*

MIKE
You're a goddamned liar.

DOCTOR
*Come on now, Mike, I don't have to listen to that
from you.*

MIKE
The hell you don't.

Mike shows the doctor the picture that Bernard took of Martin and Barbara.

POSNER
Did you know Barbara was at that school?

The doctor rips off the barber's apron and puts on his hat and jacket.

DOCTOR
What the hell, I can see this is going no place.

POSNER
Doc, did Cole know she was at the school.

The doctor ignores Posner and stalks out of the barber-shop.

MIKE
(to the loungers)
You guys wait, just wait till it happens to one of your kids.

POSNER
Well, now I don't think we ought to wait.

SCHOOL AUDITORIUM, BACKSTAGE
INTERIOR NIGHT

The students are rushing through the final preparations for their show.

CINDY
Jean.

JEAN
Yeah?

CINDY
Telephone.

JEAN
Thank you.

Jean crosses to the phone.

KIT
Come on, you guys, Star Spangled Banner, get out here, places, come on.

JEAN
(into receiver)
Hello.

PHONE BOOTH IN TOWN   EXTERIOR   NIGHT

STUDENT
Jean, I'm afraid it's really bad. Nobody's going to show up tonight.

SCHOOL AUDITORIUM   INTERIOR   NIGHT

JEAN
Why not?

PHONE BOOTH   EXTERIOR   NIGHT

STUDENT
Posner and the Deputy, it seems they're up to something very stupid and crazy.

SCHOOL AUDITORIUM   INTERIOR   NIGHT

The students are performing for themselves; there is no audience. A group is lined up belting out "The Star Spangled Banner." Ed is sitting. Without dropping a note, one of the singers motions to Ed to stand and join them. Ed is comfortable in his chair. Another singer turns to Ed, insisting he stand and sing. Ed refuses, and the group begins to hit and kick him. Ed tumbles to the floor, and the singers stomp him into the ground without interrupting their fervent rendition of the anthem. Ed lies motionlessly. As the group rings out with the last line, "In the land of the free, and the home of the brave," one of the singers spits at Ed.

SCHOOL EXTERIOR   NIGHT

Cole sits in a parked police car, looking toward the school. Posner, Bernard, and Mike, in a car coming down the road, spot Cole and stop at a distance.

> **COLE**
> (*projecting*)
> *Don't get out of your cars, boys. I don't want to know who any of you are. Now the only trouble we're going to have here tonight is if you try to get past me.*

SECOND CAR   INTERIOR   NIGHT

> **MIKE**
> *What do you want to do?*

> **POSNER**
> *Inch forward.*

SCHOOL EXTERIOR   NIGHT

Cole lifts his rifle from the seat.

> **COLE**
> *You all know me, you know I'm not going to let this happen. Now you just turn around and you go on back home.*

SECOND CAR   INTERIOR   NIGHT

> **BERNARD**
> (*leaning forward from the back seat*)
> *Every night Martin goes down to the barn to feed the horses. Why don't we grab him and hold him until they give you Barbara back?*

SCHOOL AUDITORIUM INTERIOR NIGHT

One of the girls is up on stage singing, as slides flash on a screen behind her. Jean is watching distractedly, troubled.

> **JEAN**
> *Cindy.*
>
> **CINDY**
> *Yes?*
>
> **JEAN**
> *Go down to the barn and get Martin, would you please?*
>
> **CINDY**
> *Okay.*

BARN INTERIOR NIGHT

Cindy comes through the door.

> **CINDY**
> (projecting)
> *Martin, Martin, come out, come out wherever you are.*

As she enters, Cindy sees Posner, Bernard, and Mike with a gun at Martin's head. Her face tightens with horror.

CANYON EXTERIOR NIGHT

Martin is being held captive. He sits on the ground. Mike kicks Martin from behind.

> **CINDY**
> *Stop it!*
>
> **POSNER**
> (to Mike)
> *I thought I told you to leave him alone.*

MIKE
I was just giving the pacifist a chance to turn the other cheek.

SCHOOL PORCH EXTERIOR DAY

Barbara listens as Cole explains again to Jean.

COLE
Jean, if I knew where they were holding him I'd go there right away. At this point they don't trust me any more than they do you.

JEAN
I couldn't possibly turn her over to that man.

COLE
Why not? She can run away again right after she gets there. In the meantime the boy will be safe.

JEAN
Cole, you know damn well Posner will never hurt that boy. Wouldn't you arrest him if he did?

COLE
Sure, I'd arrest him. But we can't get a conviction in this town and you know it.

Barbara steps off the porch toward Jean and Cole.

BARBARA
I'm going back with you. He's right. As long as I'm sitting here anything could happen—and as soon as Martin's safe, I can split again.

JEAN
(looks helplessly at Cole)
What can I say?

CANYON EXTERIOR DAY

Time is moving slowly. Bored, Mike steps in front of Martin and slaps him.

> **MIKE**
> (an afterthought)
> *All right, Buck, where is she?*

The others have lost interest. Unnoticed, Cindy edges toward a rifle in the truck. She lunges, grabs the rifle and holds it on Mike.

> **CINDY**
> *Leave him alone.*

> **MIKE**
> (his voice not as sure as the words)
> *She can't pull that trigger.*

> **CINDY**
> (pleading)
> *You release that boy or I swear I'll shoot you. I swear it. Please don't make me shoot you.*

Mike approaches her, one step at a time.

> **MIKE**
> *Now look, miss, do you have the courage to shoot a man that's looking you right in the eye?*

> **CINDY**
> *Please don't make me shoot you. Please.*

As Mike continues to advance, Cindy shoots, kicking up four spurts of dust at Mike's feet. All her attention is on Mike and Cindy does not see the man circling behind her.

> **MARTIN**
> *Look out!*

Cindy spins and snaps off a shot in the man's direction. He stops.

102

CINDY
Martin, get in the truck.

Martin climbs into the cab.

MARTIN
Okay, come on, get in.

CINDY
(still facing the men)
No, they'll follow you.

MARTIN
I can't leave without you.

CINDY
Martin, get going. Soon as you're gone, it's all over with. Now go back to the school.

MARTIN
I can't.

CINDY
Martin, please get going.

Martin hesitates another moment, then reluctantly drives away. Cindy holds the rifle on the men, now spread out. Uncertainly, she tries to account for any who might be missing. As Cindy turns slowly, she is struck from behind. The rifle is torn from her hands.

POSNER
All right, Bernard. Go get him.

Bernard and Dinosaur scoop up their rifles and jump into the Corvette.

POSNER
Careful, he's armed!

SCHOOL   EXTERIOR   DAY

Kit roars up in the jeep.

KIT
Jean! Jean! Billy's gone after Martin!

JEAN
Oh, Lord, no.

ROADSIDE EXTERIOR DAY

Martin drives the truck frantically along the road, cutting through the woods. He cannot shake the Corvette. The road bends toward the shore of the lake. In the rearview mirror Martin sees the Corvette gaining. Martin swings onto the shoulder of the road and abandons the truck. He takes the rifle, firms his crutch under his armpit and hobbles through the woods, hoping to lose Bernard and Dinosaur in the forest. The Corvette brakes to a stop behind the truck and Bernard and Dinosaur spill out. Bernard sees Martin disappear among the trees and squeezes off a shot.

LAKESIDE EXTERIOR DAY

Bernard's bullet bites into the bark near Martin's head. Martin drops for cover, lifts the stock to his shoulder, and fires.

ROADSIDE EXTERIOR DAY

Martin's shot sprays chips off a boulder.

BERNARD
(amazed)
Well, I'll be goddamned. That Injun is shooting back.

CANYON EXTERIOR DAY

Posner suddenly makes up his mind on what to do with Cindy.

POSNER
Take her home.

MIKE
No sir, not till we get Martin back. She's all the insurance I've got.

Eerily, Billy materializes on his horse. Taken unawares, Posner and Mike are slow to react.

BILLY
Where's Martin?
(beat)
I said, where's Martin?

CINDY
He got away.

Mike pretends to look away, and under the cover of the feint, draws his gun and holds the barrel at Cindy's temple.

MIKE
(a bit too loudly)
Hold it! Now you drop that gun or I'll shoot her. I'm not going to ask you again.

BILLY
(quietly)
You won't have to.

MIKE
What?

BILLY
I said shoot her.

MIKE
You'd kill her just like that, huh?

BILLY
No, you'll kill her.

Billy slowly swings his rifle and points it at Mike.

BILLY
And then I'll kill you, just like that. I'm itching to kill somebody so it might just as well be you. Pull the trigger.

Mike laughs nervously and puts his gun away.

MIKE

I wasn't going to hurt the little girl. You knew that all the time, didn't you, buck?

BILLY
All right, Cindy. On.

Cindy steps to Billy's side, takes his hand and swings up behind him.

ROAD EXTERIOR DAY

The Sheriff and his men are searching the woods along the lake. Barbara is with them. Cole has been listening to a man he found on the scene.

COLE
Did you see anyone with a gun?

MAN
I only heard the shots.

COLE
And then what happened?

MAN
I saw a Corvette pull out.

COLE
Where'd the shots come from?

MAN
They came from over there.

LAKESIDE EXTERIOR DAY

Barbara has wandered down to the lake. Martin's crutches drift by. Shaken, Barbara follows the current and sees Martin floating, face down, in a spreading stain of blood.

LAKESIDE EXTERIOR DAY

Martin's sheet-covered body is rolled into the ambulance on a stretcher. The door is slammed and the ambulance drives off.

POSNER
Was he shot?

COLE
Four times ... in the head. I'll give you twenty-four hours to bring him in Stuart, then I'm coming after him.

POLICEMAN
Cole, the girl's gone.

PORCH EXTERIOR DAY

Cindy, Jean, and several of the students are on the porch. Billy Jack sits off to the side.

Barbara silently walks up and goes inside the building.

CINDY
It's my fault.
(beat)
It is my fault. If I would have said something, Martin wouldn't have had to die.

BOY
If you had said what? You're not making any sense.

JEAN
(trying to hush Cindy)
Cindy!

BILLY
(without looking up)
If she would have told me that Bernard raped Jean.

JEAN
How did you know?

BILLY
I didn't.

Billy gets up and walks rapidly toward his motorcycle. Jean runs after him.

JEAN
Billy please! We haven't crossed over that thin line yet, but if you kill Bernard you'll be doing just what they want. Can't you see that? You just can't keep making your own laws. There's got to be one set of laws fair for everyone including you.

BILLY
That's fine. When that set of laws is fairly applied to everyone, then I'll turn the other cheek too.

JEAN
There's got to be a better way to change those people.

BILLY
Change those people? You worked with King, didn't you?

JEAN
Yes.

BILLY
Where is he?

JEAN
Dead.

BILLY
And where's Bob and Jack Kennedy?

JEAN
Dead.

BILLY
Their brains blown out because your people wouldn't even put the same controls on their guns as they do on their dogs, their bicycles, their cats and their automobiles.

Jean is desperate to stop Billy.

JEAN
I don't care about all that. I just don't want you to go out and commit murder. Please, Billy, please. We'll go someplace else, someplace where it doesn't have to be like this.

BILLY
Oh really? Tell me where is that place? Where is it? In what remote corner of this country—no the entire goddamned planet—is there such a place where men really care about another and really love each other? Now you tell me where such a place is and I promise you that I'll never hurt another human being as long as I live. Just one place!

Jean doesn't know how to reply. Silently, she shakes her head.

BILLY
That's what I thought. I'll be back for Barbara.

Billy rides off on his motorcycle. Jean looks after him, not sure she'll ever see Billy again.

MOTEL ROOM   INTERIOR   DAY

The door is thrown open. Billy steps into the room. Bernard, in bed with a young Indian girl, looks up, startled.

> **BILLY**
> (to the girl)
> How old are you?

> **GIRL**
> Thirteen.

> **BILLY**
> Get out.

The girl covers herself with the sheet and runs out. Bernard reaches for his gun and holds it on Billy. Billy advances slowly, his deep hate making him indifferent to the threat of Bernard's gun. Terrified, Bernard jerks the trigger and misses. Billy keeps coming on. Bernard pulls himself together and fires again, hitting Billy in the side. Without breaking stride, Billy snaps a single, violent karate chop into Bernard's neck. Bernard crumples like a broken doll into the sheets.

SCHOOL EXTERIOR DAY

The school is surrounded by police, police cars and motorcycles, and state troopers. A few reporters have been drawn by the activity.

Cole is handing Jean a series of documents.

> **COLE**
> Search warrant federal, search warrant state, search warrant county and a court order demanding that Barbara be turned over to the court pending investigation into her father's fitness as a parent.

Jean stares helplessly at the documents.

DORMITORY INTERIOR DAY

110

Barbara, Cindy, and Kit are looking out the dormitory window. Billy enters the room soundlessly.

CINDY
Let's get out of here.

As she turns, Cindy steps into Billy.

BILLY
(quietly, to Barbara)
What do you want to do?

BARBARA
Go with you.

BILLY
Well, we can try.

Billy and Barbara leave. Cindy looks down at her hand. It is covered with blood from Billy's wound.

SCHOOL EXTERIOR DAY

Billy and Barbara are crossing the school grounds. Mike, inside a building facing the grounds, lifts his rifle and fires. The round bites into the building behind Billy and Barbara. Billy crouches and zigzags to the cover of a truck, pulling Barbara with him. Mike fires again. Billy reaches for a rifle on the seat in the cab of the truck. Mike empties his weapon and pauses a moment to reload. Billy steps clear of the truck, takes aim, and shoots Mike through the head. Scooping up several boxes of cartridges from the cab, Billy runs with Barbara into the nearest building, an abandoned church.

SCHOOL EXTERIOR DAY

Cole, Jean, the doctor, and several policemen are in the schoolyard. There is a great deal of activity around them—photographers, newspapermen, troopers, etc.

COLE
(into his car mike)
Tell him I'll take care of it right away.

Cole hangs the mike on its hook.

DOCTOR
(walking up, to Cole)
Well it went out over the wire services, it's a big story.

COLE
The Governor's sent someone to take personal charge. He wants everything frozen till he gets here.

POLICEMAN
(reporting to Cole)
They've cornered him in the old church. He's killed Mike.

COLE
Oh no.

DOCTOR
Well, what are we going to do, Jean? He'll die before he gives himself up.

Cole looks at Jean thoughtfully for a moment, then:

COLE
Can you talk to him? Try?

CHURCH INTERIOR DAY

The inside of the church has been barricaded. Billy Jack rubs a feather across the back of his hand, then drops several strange objects into a small leather pouch.

BARBARA
You never told me what's in that thing.

Billy runs the feather along the pouch.

BILLY
It's my medicine bag. I've got some owl's feathers, sacred corn, snake teeth.

BARBARA
What's it for?

BILLY
(smiles)
It contains my power. Without it I'd be outside of the flow of life's forces.

BARBARA
Like Samson without his hair?

BILLY
You got it.

CHURCH EXTERIOR DAY

The church is surrounded by police cars, troopers, deputies, the press, spectators, and youngsters from the school.

COLE
(over bullhorn)
Billy! Billy Jack! Can you hear me? Jean is coming in to talk to you. It's no trick. No one will try to sneak up on you, she just wants to talk to you.

CHURCH INTERIOR DAY

A few moments later. Jean hasn't taken her eyes off Billy since she came into the church but doesn't know what to say.

JEAN
I don't suppose you care too much that you're bleeding to death.

BILLY
Everything they want from here on out they're

going to have to take. You don't understand that, do
you?

JEAN
No. I only know you can't solve everything by violence, Billy.

There is the sound of wailing sirens. Jean walks to the
window, looks out, then turns back to Billy.

JEAN
(turns to Billy, weeping softly)
They'll kill you, Billy. I wish there was something I
could say to change all that. I know I've never said
it to you . . . but I think you know . . . I love you.

Without looking at Jean, Billy nods to indicate his feelings.

BILLY
I think you know too.

JEAN
(crying)
It just seems so insane that we have to go on living
without you.
(tears choke her)
What about Barbara?

BILLY
It's up to her to decide.

JEAN
Barbara, will you go out with me?

BARBARA
No.

JEAN
May I ask why?

BARBARA
From the day I was born, to this moment, and every

second in between, life has just been one big shit brick. I just can't take it anymore. And the way things are going ... well as the Indians say, "Today is as good as any to die."

JEAN
(to Billy)
You've taught her well.

BILLY
An Indian isn't afraid to die. Don't ever expect a white man to understand that.

JEAN
I understand it. It's good—for an Indian.

BILLY
Like the old man said, being an Indian is not a matter of blood, it's a way of life.

JEAN
I understand that too.
(anger clears the tears from Jean's voice)
But she's a fifteen-year-old child who worships the ground you walk on. And now she's going to die needlessly because you haven't got the guts to control your temper.

Billy doesn't respond. Jean knows she hasn't changed his mind—and can't.

JEAN
It's so easy for you to die dramatically. It's a hell of a lot tougher for those of us who have to keep on trying.

Jean walks out the door.

CHURCH EXTERIOR DAY

A helicopter lands with several officials—including Charlie and Jim from the Governor's office. Armed troopers and police swarm about. The size of the crowd has increased. Nearby, a television crew is setting up.

> **COLE**
> *Hello, Charlie. How are you Jim?*

> **CHARLIE**
> *What's the situation?*

> **COLE**
> *He's barricaded himself in the church.*

> **CHARLIE**
> *We must make every attempt to take him alive.*

> **COLE**
> *No way.*

> **CHARLIE**
> *He's only one man, it shouldn't be too tough.*

> **JIM**
> *What do you mean no way? Why can't you just move on in there and take him with some cover fire, then bring him out with some tear gas. You've got a whole army here.*

> **COLE**
> *No way.*

> **CHARLIE**
> *Can you do it?*

> **STATE TROOPER**
> *We can do it.*

REAR OF CHURCH EXTERIOR DAY

State troopers and policemen swarm about the church, armed with a variety of weapons. Silently, they take cover.

At a prearranged signal they open fire, blanketing the church with a fusilade of rifle and small arms fire.

CHURCH INTERIOR DAY

As the bullets rip into the church, Billy slams Barbara to the floor behind a shield of tables and bunks he has built for her.

> **BILLY**
> *Get down.*

As Billy moves toward the window, Barbara moves to get up.

> **BARBARA**
> *I want to help load.*

> **BILLY**
> *Stick your head up and I'll knock it off.*

The firing outside grows heavier. Billy moves from one window to another, returning fire with the loaded rifles he placed at each position. He ducks as bullets shatter the glass, ricocheting off walls and splintering furniture. Then there is a momentary lull. Billy swivels into firing position and pulls the trigger.

CHURCH EXTERIOR DAY

A trooper, trying to move closer with tear gas, is hit and sprawls into the dirt.

> **CHARLIE**
> *(over bullhorn)*
> *Pull back! Pull back! Cease fire! Cease fire! Cease fire! Pull back!*

CHURCH INTERIOR DAY

> **BILLY**
> *Okay, you can come out now.*

BARBARA

I don't think I can.

Billy rushes over to her. She has been shot in the leg, but smiles up at him through her pain.

BARBARA

This darn stuff's not all its cracked up to be.

Billy admires her courage.

BILLY

Oh you crazy nut.

CHURCH INTERIOR DAY

Hospital aides are taking Barbara out on a stretcher. Billy's rifle follows them. Jean stands off to the side.

BARBARA

Don't let them take me.

Billy waves the aides aside with the muzzle of the rifle and comes over to Barbara.

BILLY

You don't even have a medicine bag, so how can it be your day to die? You're going. Period.

BARBARA

It's just that if you die, that'll kill Jean and the school and everything she lives for, and, if you love her, I don't see why you do that to her. That's all.

Billy hugs Barbara, holding her tightly as she kisses his cheek. He releases her and the aides step forward. They lift the stretcher and carry Barbara out.

CHURCH EXTERIOR NIGHT

CHARLIE
We've got to take him alive. Where's that girl?

STATE TROOPER
She's already been in there several times.

CHARLIE
Well, then send her in several more.

COLE
Maybe a couple of us ought to go in there with her this time.

CHURCH EXTERIOR NIGHT

A few moments later. Jean, the doctor and Cole approach the church door and stop.

COLE
(projecting)
Hey, Billy. We're not armed. No tricks, you have my word.

BILLY
Come ahead.

CHURCH INTERIOR NIGHT

Billy sits listening, but unconvinced.

DOCTOR
... but you will get a fair trial. Because the whole world will have reporters here watching it, and because a lot of politicians will realize it's in their own selfish interests to at least go through the form of giving you a fair trial. But in the meantime you will have accomplished an awful lot of good.

BILLY
Like what?

DOCTOR
*Like calling attention to the unbelievably horrible
way that the Indians are cheated and forced to live
in this country, and the stupid insensitivity of Washington and the whole Indian bureau.*

COLE
*For God sakes, Billy, if you get killed now, it's a
headline in tomorrow's paper. But if you go to trial,
millions of people will learn what's happening.*

BILLY
(still skeptical)
*Like you just said, not a damn thing will be done
about it.*

JEAN
(to the doctor)
*What about the school? Could we get enough money
and freedom to run it for the next five years without
any interference?*

DOCTOR
They'd give you that in a minute.

JEAN
In writing?

COLE
I'm sure they would.

BILLY
*It's funny, isn't it? Only the white man wants every-
thing put in writing and then only so he can use it
against you in court. You know, among the Indians
a promise is good enough. As far as I can tell,
Washington entered into 3,500 treaties with the Indians to date and they've broken about 3,499 of them.*

COLE
I agree with you, Billy, promises haven't meant very

much. But this is one they'll keep. The important point is this, if you have to go out, you might as well make it count for something.

(beat)

Well, I can't think of anything else to say.

The room is silent, then:

BILLY

Tell them that I'll give them an answer in the morning.

Sheriff Cole and the doctor leave.

BILLY

(to Jean)

We're different, you and I. Your spirit is more calm and pacific in you than any person I've ever known. And mine has been in a violent rage from the day that I was born. And you know something, I didn't really want it that way.

JEAN

Billy, that's a bunch of crap. I'm no different than you. Do you think when Bernard was on top of me grunting and slobbering, I didn't hate? I hated more than anybody else on this earth ever hated and every time that picture pops into my mind. . . .

(fights for control, then, without emotion)

I've never hated so much in my life. When I think of that, I dismember and mangle and I castrate Bernard over and over in my mind at least a million times a day. The bad part is even though he's dead I couldn't tell you: you could get your hate out. I had to keep mine in.

(they look at each other for a long time)

I knew what you would do. I knew how important it was to the kids, and I knew that their lives and their needs were more important than any hate I had, were more important than killing Bernard. But

> *maybe, maybe if I had told you, Martin might be*
> *alive now.*
> (beat)
> *I don't know. I don't know anymore.*

Jean leaves.

CHURCH EXTERIOR DAY

Jean comes out of the church and faces Charlie.

> **JEAN—**
> *He wants these conditions. First, that the school be*
> *guaranteed to operate for the next ten years without*
> *any interference and that I be given a ten year con-*
> *tract as Directress. Second, that Barbara be put in*
> *my custody as her legal guardian.*

> **CHARLIE**
> *That all he wants?*

> **JEAN**
> *No. He also wants you to guarantee that someone*
> *from the governor's office will hold a press confer-*
> *ence every year to announce the progress of the*
> *school.*

> **CHARLIE**
> *He's got it.*
> (to Jim)
> *Call Washington and make sure they'll honor their*
> *end of the bargain.*

Jean turns back toward the church.

CHURCH INTERIOR DAY

Billy sits silently, leaning on his rifle.

> **JEAN**
> *Some lawyer called from the East. He wants to de-*
> *fend you free.*

There is a long pause. Billy stands and places his gun on the table. Jean can't hold her tears.

JEAN
I know to let them handcuff you, close you in and lock you up is by far the hardest thing you've ever done. And I know that you're only doing it because of the love you have for the kids. . . and me.

Billy walks over to Jean, takes her in his arms and holds her.

CHARLIE
(v. o.)
Washington says okay, Billy.

JEAN
(crying)
I love you, Billy.

CHARLIE
(v. o.)
You've got a deal.

Billy and Jean hold each other tightly.

CHURCH EXTERIOR DAY

Students, Indians, kids, and townspeople are pressing around the entrance to the church as Billy and Jean come out. Cole steps forward. Light bulbs flash. Billy holds up his wrists and the sheriff snaps on the handcuffs. Billy examines the iron pinning his hands, looks up at Cole, then steps forward, Cole at his side. Jean remains at the church. Leading Cole, Billy stops beside a police car. He hesitates a moment, then bends in. The door slams and the car starts forward.

ROAD EXTERIOR DAY

The road is lined as far as the eye can see by students and

Indians, some standing, others hunkered down. As the police car approaches, a girl wheels to face it and raises a clenched fist in the power-to-the-people salute. One by one, on both sides of the road, the kids and Indians step forward, raising their fists as the car with Billy speeds by.

> (song over)
> Listen, children, to a story
> That was written long ago
> About a kingdom on a mountain
> And a valley far below. . . .

Churning dust, the police car disappears in the distance. The song slowly fades.

> (song over)
> There won't be any trumpets blowing
> Come the judgment day
> On the bloody morning after
> One tin soldier rides away.

FADE OUT